Voyages Out 1:

Lesbian Short Fiction

**by Paula Martinac
and Carla Tomaso**

The Seal Press

Acknowledgements

My special thanks go to Maureen Brady, Catherine Dillon, Suzanne Seay, Barbara Selfridge, and Barbara Wilson for their help with these stories.

Paula Martinac

My thanks to Mary Hayden, Naomi Sehely, Elizabeth Brosnahan-Broome and Barbara Wilson.

Carla Tomaso

Cover design by Clare Conrad.

We gratefully acknowledge the following for permission to reprint previously published works:

Paula Martinac: "Like Mother, Like. . . " originally appeared in *We Are Everywhere: Writings by and about Lesbian Parents*, edited by Harriet Alpert (Crossing Press, 1988); "The Tenants" was first published in *conditions* 15 (Fall, 1988); "Mineola, Mineola" first appeared in *Sinister Wisdom* 38 (Summer, 1989).

Carla Tomaso: "Kat" originally appeared in *Common Lives, Lesbian Lives*; "Tattoo" was first published in *Unholy Alliances*, edited by Louise Rafkin (Cleis Press, 1988); "Avalon" originally appeared in *Bachy*.

Library of Congress Cataloging-in-Publication Data

Martinac, Paula, 1954–
    Lesbian short fiction / Paula Martinac, Carla Tomaso.
        p.   cm. — (Voyages out ; 1)
    ISBN 0-931188-79-2
    1. Lesbians—Fiction. 2. Lesbians' writings, American. 3. Short stories, American—Women authors. I. Tomaso, Carla. II. Title. III. Series
PS648.L47M38   1989
813'.54—dc20   89-10206
ISSN: 1043-948X   CIP

Printed in the United States of America
First printing, September 1989
10 9 8 7 6 5 4 3 2 1

Seal Press
P.O. Box 13
Seattle, WA 98111

VOYAGES OUT 1

PAULA MARTINAC

Mineola, Mineola	3
The Tenants	11
Strangers in the Night	15
Cysters	28
Like Mother, Like...	34
A Matter of Convenience	47
Sex Among the Bukovacs	55
Shelter	63

CARLA TOMASO

Kat	71
I Love You More Than Anything	81
Tattoo	93
Avalon	105
My Father, the Novelist	115
Stranger	121

Voyages Out 1

Paula Martinac

Mineola, Mineola

In Charleston, West Virginia, on Quarrier Street, there is a big old house that used to belong to my great-grandmother Wycke. It was built around 1905, when she and my great-granddaddy were married. They had quite a lot of money then. My great-granddaddy was a lawyer, in a long line of lawyers, right on back to the American Revolution. But he was kind of a dreamer, too, like the first Wyckes who trudged across the Appalachians into western Virginia in the early 1800s to try to make their fortunes. Great-granddaddy took off suddenly in the 1920s for New York, because, he said, he just needed to try something new. He took his secretary with him. He left my great-grandmother with three boys and the house on Quarrier Street. Her family helped her out as long as they could, but then came the Depression and West Virginia was hit pretty badly. Great-grandmother sold the house to a politician. Now, over fifty years later, the house has been divided into three apartments, one on each floor. When I first heard the story, I was just a kid and I would go and stare at the house and fantasize that I lived there. It was years before I found out that I was staring at the wrong house. One day my daddy and I were driving along Quarrier Street on our way downtown and I said, pointing to the house, "I just love that big old house where your grandmother lived."

"That's not the one," my daddy said. "It's a few doors

down." The real house was even bigger and grander, with a leaded glass window over the door set in a sunrise pattern. In a few weeks, I forgot I'd ever stared at any other house.

So I guess I'm a bit of a dreamer, too, and that's why things have happened to me the way they have. I've dreamed about living in big houses and seeing the ocean and being a famous writer with a hit play on Broadway. But until I followed Leah to Mineola, I had never been out of West Virginia, except once to visit my second cousins in Lexington, Kentucky, and that doesn't really count.

When I met her, Leah and her two friends were on their way back from a cross-country camping trip. They were getting tired of their adventure and were stopping in cities, checking into motels, looking up relatives so they wouldn't have to sleep outside. One of the women had a cousin in Charleston, and they were all staying with him for a few days. I met Leah by accident in the express line at Kroger's. I kept stealing glances at her over my shoulder, because she had the shortest hair I'd ever seen on a woman, misty grey eyes, and one silver earring in a design I'd just become familiar with recently. She was definitely not from Charleston, I could tell that right away. When she noticed me looking at her, she smiled and ran a hand across her hair.

"Do I know you from somewhere?" Then she blushed and looked at her feet for a moment. "I know that sounds like a line, but you look so familiar. Did you used to wait tables at Network, by any chance?"

"No," I said. "Is that in town?"

She blushed again. "No, that's a bar in New York City. You look like one of the waitresses there, but your hair's a little longer."

"No," I said again, "I've never been to New York." The checkout person rang up my milk, hamburger buns and mustard. "You from New York?" I asked to keep the conversation going.

"Yeah," she said, fingering a silver necklace that matched the earring. "I work in Manhattan, and I live out on Long Island."

"Near the ocean?" I asked, picturing my great-grandmother's house perched on a hill overlooking the raging Atlantic.

"Sort of," she smiled.

As the checker bagged my groceries, I decided to be bold and comment on the earring. "I couldn't help noticing your earring. It's real pretty." I picked up my bag but wasn't ready to leave yet. I had taken a real chance, I thought, but what could I lose by being forward with someone from out of town?

"Wait a minute," she said, as she paid for her orange juice. "I'll walk out with you." I stood there obediently, my heart pounding in my chest.

I remembered that Reva, my roommate, had a pair of sweat socks with the same entwined women's symbols on them, meaning that she was gay. She'd gotten them through a mail-order catalog. I had wondered why she wanted to announce she was gay on her socks like that, and she said it was so other gay women could spot her. Reva had said maybe that's why I wasn't getting any action, because I wasn't making announcements. But mostly I wasn't "getting any action" because I was scared. I'd never been with a woman before, though I'd been thinking about it since I was in high school.

Now here I was walking out of Kroger's with a gay woman from New York City. "Are you from here?" she was asking me. When I nodded, she continued, "Then you must know where the bars are. I'm here for a few days with friends, and we only found one that was mostly men."

It was funny, I thought, how in one simple acknowledgment of her earring, she'd known I was gay. It was really a network, just like Reva always said. Now it was going to be hard to follow up. I had only been to the women's bar in Charleston a couple of times but wanted to act like a seasoned regular.

"Yeah, it's over on Morris Street," I said. "I'll draw you a map, if you've got a pen."

"Better yet, maybe you could come with us," she smiled, opening up her orange juice carton and offering me some. "My friends and I wanted to go tonight. How about it?" She took a big drink, then smiled embarrassedly. "Here I am, inviting you out and you don't even know my name. I'm Leah Shane."

"I'm Cass Wycke," I said, holding out my hand, which was sweaty with nervousness, "and I would love to go with you."

I don't know how I got up the courage to ask her to leave the bar with me, but it probably had something to do with the three gin-and-tonics I had. She was drinking beer and telling stories about all the women they'd met going cross-country. Camping cross-country seemed like the most romantic thing to do, and I was already saying, "I'll have to try that sometime," forgetting that my friends were not the camping type. Maybe it was the fact that she flirted outrageously with me and no one had ever really done that before. She rubbed her knee against mine under the table, put her arm across the back of my chair, touched my arm as she told a story. She wore a tight black t-shirt with the word "Lesberado" across the front. And her eyes, which looked, I thought, like the mist rising out of the ocean, were so penetrating I felt a little hypnotized by them. She talked authoritatively about New York and whispered encouragingly, "You really should come to New York sometime. You'd love it. We could see a play together. Have you seen 'La Cage aux Folles'? Then we could hit the dance clubs." It seemed more like a proposal of marriage than an invitation dropped casually in a bar. So when it looked like they were

getting ready to leave, and with them most of the excitement I'd known in the last few years, I leaned toward Leah's
ear and said, "Would you like to come back to my apartment? It's not much, and I share it with a friend, but she'll
be asleep."

I didn't have to ask twice. And I didn't mention that,
even though I was twenty-one and had been on my own for
two years, I'd never had sex with anyone, man or woman. I
hoped she wouldn't notice and that the drinks I'd had would
give me the nerve to try out some of the things I'd
memorized from Reva's *Joy of Lesbian Sex* book. I didn't
have to worry too much. She was all over me, and I just followed her lead. Whatever she did to me, I did to her, just
changing it slightly so she wouldn't think I was copying. It
was better than I ever dreamed, sexier than the pictures in
Reva's book. I knew from the steamy novels I read as a kid
that you were supposed to make lots of noise if you were
having a good time, and I did that, too. I don't think Leah
guessed my secret, because before we fell asleep, she said,
"You Southern girls sure are something else."

It makes me blush to think we stayed in bed for almost
two days, but we did. We got up to eat and take showers
and then went right back to bed. Reva winked at me once as
I cut through the kitchen back to my room, but we didn't
talk about it till later. On Sunday afternoon, Leah got up
and started to get dressed.

"This must be what they mean by a lost weekend," she
smiled, pulling on her jeans and t-shirt. She sat on the edge
of the bed to put on her sneakers. "So when are you coming
to New York?" she asked with a smile.

"Soon, I hope," I said, quietly realizing that she was leaving.

"Let me give you the number in Mineola," Leah offered,
scouring the room for pen and paper. "If you ever make it
up my way, you can give me a call."

The leaving was not like I imagined. I thought she'd hug me tightly and ask me to come along, say that she couldn't stand to be one night without me. Instead she hugged me and brushed the hair out of my eyes. "Here's looking at you, kid," she said, but I had never seen that movie, and Reva had to explain it to me later.

I got a postcard from her about ten days later as she wound her way up the East Coast. It was from Rehoboth Beach, which she said was a little gay paradise. I figured out approximately when she would be back in New York. Reva tried to talk me out of it, but I decided to take a few extra days off from work in a couple of weeks and go to New York over the Labor Day weekend, surprise Leah. Then I thought I'd better not surprise her, in case she had plans, and I sent her a postcard detailing my trip, saying I would love to see "La Cage aux Folles," if she could get tickets. I tried to call her a couple of times before I left to confirm the plans, but she wasn't home.

I guess it was crazy to go but I went anyway. I told Reva I was going to visit my aunt in Beckley. I took the train, which was almost a fifteen-hour trip, including transfers. Most of it was at night, though, so it wasn't so bad. I did mind missing all the scenery, but I figured there would be plenty of time for that on the way back. And I knew that once I saw the Manhattan skyline, once I'd breathed the ocean air on Long Island, once I saw Leah, I wouldn't regret the trip one bit.

It was early on Saturday morning when I got on the Long Island Railroad to Mineola. It was further from Manhattan than Leah had let on, and I marveled at how she could make the commute every day. I was used to the ten-minute walk from my apartment to the state office building where I was a word processor. I kept worrying that I would miss the stop, but the conductor called "Mineola, Mineola" right in front of me, as if he'd read my mind.

At the station stop I called the number scratched in Leah's unfamiliar hand onto a piece of notebook paper.

"Leah?" I asked breathlessly, looking around and wondering where the ocean was exactly. All I could see were dismal row houses against a heavy grey sky.

"No, she's not home right now. Who's this?"

I hesitated, thrown by the fact that she lived with someone and that she was not there to welcome me to New York. "This is Cass Wycke, a friend of hers from West Virginia. I'm at the train station. . . . "

"Oh, yeah, Cass!" the woman said, cheerfully. "She left a message for you. Hang on. . . . She got invited to Fire Island at the last minute for the weekend and won't be around to see you. Says she's sorry and hopes you have a good time."

I stared at the row houses beyond the station, wondering if I had known this would happen all along. I couldn't even smell the ocean, just a faint odor of car exhaust. Mineola, I decided then and there, didn't look much more interesting than towns I'd seen in West Virginia. "That's it?" I said.

"I guess so. I mean, yeah, that's all it says here," the woman answered, unconvincingly fumbling over her words.

"Thanks," I said, hanging up. At least, I thought, she could have left tickets for "La Cage aux Folles."

I didn't start crying till I was back on the train to Manhattan. If I'd known where Fire Island was, I'd have followed her there just to embarrass her, to demand an apology. But then, I thought, an apology for what? An apology, I guess, for not living up to my expectations, for not having a house on the beach, for not equating sex with simple kindness and caring.

I intended to go right back home, I thought that would show her. But when I stepped outside Pennsylvania Station and saw Madison Square Garden, the Empire State Building, all the places I'd heard about, I decided I might as well spend the day. I spent too much for a hotel room and much too much for a ticket to "La Cage aux Folles," which I liked pretty well. Then, to make the evening complete, I looked up "Network" under "Bars" in the phone book, but it wasn't listed, and I didn't know the names of any other women's clubs.

Just before I left in the morning, I wrote Leah a note on a hotel postcard: "Mineola's not so hot, and neither are you." But I didn't send it. I got to thinking about something Reva said once, after she'd been dumped by this girl, Holly. They'd been going out for a whole year, and one day Holly announced she was in love with someone else. Reva took it pretty well. She went out a lot, and let friends fix her up on blind dates. When I asked her if she wasn't hurt and mad, she said, "Sure, but living well's the best revenge." So when I thought about that, I decided I didn't want Leah to know how upset I was. All I wanted was to get on a train, go home and talk to Reva.

THE TENANTS

So when my sister Angela died it just about broke my heart. You know we was close, just like that. She lived upstairs over twenty years. I thought I'd never want nobody living upstairs again. We was always running upstairs, downstairs. Sometimes I'd need something for my Frank's supper. Or she'd wanna use my clothesline, if she was doing sheets or something. Some nights she'd come down and have a cup of tea with me and Frank after supper. She liked talkin' to Frank, he's real smart, reads like it's going out of style. I call him the Professor. Angela's Eddie died, oh, it must be twenty-three years ago, in a bad accident in a mill over in Pittsburgh. She lived upstairs ever since. We was just like that, I'm tellin' you. It ain't been the same without her. Easter, that's the hardest. The Easter before last, that was the first without Angela. The whole family come at Easter, our three boys and Angela's girls, and Angela and me, we'd be cooking for weeks. It's too much for one person. The sausage pies, the grain pies, the Easter bread. I couldn't do it that first year, I just sat in the kitchen and cried and my Frank told everybody, Mum can't do it this year.

Our Vinnie stayed upstairs a while, after his Mary left him to run off to California with some hippie. But then he got himself a job in Jersey and it's too far to go everyday, all the way from Brooklyn. So then the apartment's empty for two, three months and my Frank says, Mum, when we gonna get somebody for the apartment? I can't argue, I gotta call Salvatore Moretti's boy Mike and have him see if he can rent it. You gotta be careful, you can't just advertise in the paper. So Mike says to me, Kay, I'll find you a nice tenant. He says, how much for the place? I say three hundred. He says Jesus, Mary and Joseph, you're crazy, this is New York City. You could be getting five, six hundred, he says. I said, I just want nice people, maybe if we don't charge so much, we get nice people to move in and stay. I don't like it, people moving every year or two. It's too much. My sister, she lived here over twenty years. The Sabatinis, they been on the top floor now six years. Frank and me, we always say if you can't have family living upstairs, you gotta pick people who are gonna stay put a while.

So what do you think? Next week Mike brung me two girls. Nice-lookin' girls, both blondes, almost look like sisters, not more than thirty, I'd say. They both have steady jobs, they work in the city. They're good friends, you can tell they're close, just like that. They seem real quiet, polite. Well, I take one look at them and I say you can move in whenever you want. They like the apartment, they can't believe how nice it is, compared to the dumps they seen. We keep the place up nice, even when nobody was living there. Frank, he wanted to make some improvements like we did downstairs, put in a drop ceiling to cover up that old-fashioned tin, maybe some new paneling in the living room, but I said no, let's leave it how Angela had it. The girls seemed to like it that way, they say it must be real old. Belonged to my grandmother, I say, next year it'll be a hundred years old. I tell them there's no roaches here, we mind our own business, we don't bother nobody. I'm praying these nice girls take the apartment. Well, they call the next day, the real quiet one Christine calls, she takes care of all the business stuff, and she come over to give me the deposit. She always pays the rent, too, all in cash, right on the day, not two weeks later like some tenants. I tell everybody I'm so lucky I got such nice tenants. So quiet, you almost never hear them. They stick together pretty much, they're not always having people over. Leave together in the morning, come home together. Even went, where did they go, some beach together on vacation. Susan, she's the younger one, she's a real firecracker. So much personality, I call her my girlfriend and she thinks that's funny. She always says how nice I look, asks if I got a new dress. She's a pistol all right, she makes the quiet one laugh a lot. A couple of times they have tea with me at night, but mostly they keep to themselves. No men coming in and out, either, I like that. You never know these days.

Our Vinnie says, Mum, why ain't they married, girls that old? Nice-lookin' girls, too. Vinnie, he don't know nothin' about girls like this. These girls are different, they ain't from around here, they're from the Midwest someplace, they're what you call career girls. These girls talk like they're educated, even better than the Professor. It's different nowadays. Girls don't get married right away like they used to. Me, I never finished high school even. I married my Frank when I was just seventeen, 'cause he was shipping out, you know, during the war. Everybody did that. Around here if you didn't get a husband by the time you was twenty-one, people called you an old maid. Girls don't do that no more. All that women's lib stuff. Now they wait till they're thirty, forty even to get married. Everything's different now. These girls, they're women's libbers.

Well, it was about a year after they come here when my Frank started to say that he didn't see Susan so much anymore, where was Susan? I started to notice it, too, and I asked Christine. She said, oh, Susan's working hard, away on business a lot. I'm startin' to wonder, are they doing okay? I'd run into Christine on the stairs and say, where's my girlfriend, where's that Susan? Finally, I see Susan and she says, yeah, she's working all the time, she's been out of town. But I get worried, I think maybe Christine gets lonely up there all by herself. She don't seem no different, maybe a little more quiet. Then one night I heard crying upstairs and loud voices, must have been pretty loud, 'cause you don't usually hear nothin' with this drop ceiling and all. So one day I says again, where's that Susan, and Christine says Susan's moving out, she got an apartment over on Manhattan Avenue with another girl. And I ask if she'll be okay with the rent and all, and she says I shouldn't worry, she'll be fine. Then I'm wondering if they had a fight or something to make Susan move out, and she says no, it ain't like that, they're still friends. She says Susan just wants more room, she got a bigger place for the same money. But I don't believe it. Not in this neighborhood. They was close, I'm tellin' you, just like that. I know close. I think something went wrong. I get nervous, you know, worrying that maybe Christine will get lonely and move out, too. I know how lonely you can get when somebody leaves you unexpected.

So one day I run into Susan on the street, I go out to get the paper every morning, so I decide to ask her. I think it's probably her fault, she's such a pistol, and Christine's so quiet, she hardly says boo. I say how could you leave Christine? She says Christine's fine, they're still friends. She says Christine likes to be alone, she'll be fine.

But me, I ain't so sure. I know what I heard, I heard crying upstairs. No, like the Professor says, it ain't so convincing an argument.

Strangers in the Night

On a Sunday night when she was eight years old, Margo was sitting in the middle of her circus-print bedspread talking to her stuffed dog, Sandy, and waiting for her mother to come tuck her into bed. She could hear her mother through the wall washing the dinner dishes, humming snatches of a Glenn Miller song that her father was playing on the record player downstairs in the basement. She could hear her father whistling below her room, probably dancing with himself as he often did when her mother was busy. Sometimes he would pull her mother, laughing with soapy fingers or a cooking spoon in her hand, down to the basement where they would dance together to Tommy Dorsey, Paul Whiteman, all the old bands they'd courted to, on the original 78's her father had bought as a teenager and still treasured. And her mother would forget that the sauce was boiling over or she'd left the water running until they'd dipped one final dip and reality came rushing back. "I swear, Dave Kresko, you make me act like a kid sometimes," she would half-scold, half-tease, smoothing her hair and tending to her chores again.

Her father was a good dancer. One of the most popular family stories was about her father, Dave, at nineteen, not knowing how to dance but wanting to date her mother, Marie, who was seventeen and light on her feet from years of practicing with her girlfriends. So Dave decided he would learn to dance at home with his sister Kitty, who was just fifteen. He became so good, twirling Kitty in the base ment of their house to records played on their father's Victrola, that he eventually worked up the courage to ask Marie to dance. Twenty years and three kids later, they were still dancing, at home and every Saturday night at their favorite nightclub.

Now her father started playing a new song, not one of his classic 78's, but something Margo hadn't heard before. She could hear it clearly through the floorboards, the melody strengthened by her father's whistling. "Strangers in the night, exchanging glances," came the dreamy voice of Frank Sinatra.

The song hadn't been playing long when Margo heard the water turned off in the kitchen, her mother's purposeful steps descending to the basement. She's going down to dance, Margo thought. Instead she heard the needle scraping across the record and the sound of the record snapping in half. She heard her parents screaming at each other for the first time in her life. Before she knew it, they had moved the argument upstairs, and her older sister Dottie had come into the bedroom, frightened by their unexpected and unprecedented fury. Her parents stood in the doorway of the bedroom with ugly, angry faces.

"Go ahead, tell them what's going on!" her mother screamed. "Tell them about that bleached blonde you danced with last Saturday! The one you're having an affair with. Tell them about *your* song! Go on, let your daughters know what kind of father they have!"

"Your mother's crazy," her father said venomously. "She should be locked up somewhere."

"Oh, you'd like that, wouldn't you? How convenient for you and that floozy! Your father wants you to have a new mother! Well, I can make it easy for you. I'll get a divorce. I'll move out and you can bring the dumb blonde here to raise your children!" Her mother, red in the face from screaming, pushed him out of the way roughly and went into their bedroom, slamming the door. Margo imagined her in there, crying and packing a suitcase.

Her father, equally red, left the room without another word. He went back to the basement but didn't play any records. Dottie tucked Margo in and read her a story with a quivering voice, trying to act adult even though she was only twelve. Their older brother Jack came in later and missed the incident entirely.

Later, trying to sleep, Margo heard her father's quiet knock at his own bedroom door. His low voice was too soft to make out the words. Margo, praying for a miracle, held her breath as the door opened and her father went inside. Only minutes later, it seemed, or maybe in her dreams, she heard them laughing.

No one in the family ever mentioned the argument, which was the only one of its kind in the eighteen years Margo lived at her parents' home. That was the way of the Kresko family. Yet sometimes, twenty years later, Margo still thought of it when she looked at her father.

...

Margo's mother had always said that the three Kresko children had inherited their stubbornness, and all their other bad traits, from their father. "You got that from *him*," she'd say. "No one on my side of the family was bull-headed like that. We were all nice and agreeable."

Margo was reminded of that when she and her father were driving up Sixth Avenue in his car and she instructed him, "You want to turn right here, Dad, at Houston Street."

Her father turned but studied the street sign as he did, craning his neck to make out the name. "This is Hyooston Street," he informed her.

She stiffened a little in her seat, having been through a hundred conversations just like this one. "Well, it does look like that, but New Yorkers pronounce it Howston," she said, in a pleasant, for-your-information tone.

"New Yorkers," he scoffed, "what do *they* know?"

She had not been looking forward to this visit from her father. He had never visited her alone before, always with her mother; in fact, she had never really been alone with him before, except for a few hours here and there. He had been a stranger most of her life, the man who worked long hours of overtime to pay for the mortgage and college for the kids. The basis of their relationship, ever since Margo was a teenager, had been a series of petty arguments. He was the man, after all, who had wanted to replace Mommy with a mysterious blonde. At first, Margo had started the arguments, but then her father got practiced at initiating them, too. Her mother had always acted like a buffer between them. She would have said, "Now, Dave, New Yorkers must know something, they did name the street after all." If Margo had said that, and she did think of it, the conversation would have gone on, slowly and surely developing into a no-win argument, the kind that ended in her storming out of wherever they were, even a car, saying, "I just can't talk to you, you're impossible."

So she kept quiet. She was thirty years old and tired of arguments with her father that had not changed very much in fifteen years. She had, after all, invited him to visit. And her mother was not there to cut in and say, "Isn't that a nice-looking little restaurant? Why don't you park the car, Dave, and we'll all get out and have something to eat?" This was her father's first visit to New York since her mother had died two months before. And Margo was feeling guilty now, because, in her weakest moments of grief, she had wondered why it hadn't been her father who had died instead of her mother.

When she didn't pursue the Houston Street argument, Margo's father let it drop. "How's this new apartment working out?" They stopped for a red light, and her father tensed up when two black teenagers approached the car. He seemed to relax a little when he saw they only wanted to clean his windshield.

"Oh, thanks," he said, looking sheepish.

Margo nudged his arm. "Give them some change, Dad."

"Oh," he said again, fishing in his pockets and coming up empty. The light turned green, and he pressed the gas, saying "thanks" to one of the teenagers, who shook a fist after the car.

"You really should give them something," Margo said.

"I didn't have any change," her father said, firmly. "Damn colored kids. I didn't ask them to clean my windshield." Margo swallowed hard, wondering how he would react when he met her lover Rae.

They drove the next few blocks in silence before turning at Suffolk Street. Her father's eyes widened as they passed an empty lot, an abandoned building with curtains and flowers painted on the boarded-up windows, a group of Hispanic youths drinking beer in front of the local bodega. They turned a few more corners and Margo said, "Here it is. You can park right in front of the building."

Both bottom doors to the building were wide open. Margo tried to think quickly of some excuse for why they would be. "Well, that's odd," she said, feigning confusion. "These are usually locked. Maybe someone's moving in."

Her father followed her up the flight of stairs to 2E. On the door was drawn the cartoon figure of a woman lifting weights, the work of the talented Rae.

"Someone put graffiti on your door," her father noted.

"Oh, Rae did that," Margo explained, fumbling with the difficult lock. "On purpose. We had a birthday party for her a week ago and she wanted to decorate."

Margo's father had never met Rae, though she and Margo had been lovers for over a year. The last time he'd been in New York, with Margo's mother at Thanksgiving, Rae had been visiting her sister in Philadelphia.

Rae was home now, playing an old Joan Armatrading tape, her long body sprawled over the rolled-up futon as she drew aimlessly in a sketchbook. She had spent the morning vacuuming the apartment and stashing their dirty clothes out of sight. Now she was waiting with cold beers.

"Hi, Mr. Kresko," she said, jumping up and extending an icy cold hand. "I'm Rae Richards. I'm glad we finally get to meet."

Margo's father shook her hand warily, and Margo wondered if he had ever shaken hands with a black person before. "Hi," was all he said.

Margo kissed Rae's cheek, though normally, if her father hadn't been there, she would have kissed her mouth. "Hi, babe," she said. "The place looks great."

"How about a beer, Mr. Kresko?" Rae asked, with more animation than usual.

"I don't drink," he said, abruptly, setting down his overnight bag in the corner of the living room.

Margo elaborated, "Remember, Rae, Dad's diabetes."

"Oh, sure," Rae said. "I didn't realize that meant no beer. Well, it makes sense, all that sugar," she finished nervously. Rae wandered into the kitchen and Margo followed her.

"Dad would like to go to the Intrepid today," Margo said, taking a beer for herself and a Tab for her father. "You know, the aircraft carrier. Wanna come?" They were both looking distractedly into the refrigerator.

"You gotta be kidding," Rae said. "Did you see the way he looked at me? I thought for a minute he wasn't going to shake my hand. Didn't want to dirty himself." She pushed the refrigerator door closed with determination, as though shutting Margo's father inside. "Five bucks says he doesn't talk to me at all."

Margo put her arm around Rae's shoulders. "I'm sorry. I should've known it was a bad idea for him to stay with us. I could say he'd be more comfortable at a hotel. He'd probably like that better."

"No," said Rae, her shoulders stiff under Margo's touch, "just as long as he doesn't *say* anything racist."

"Well," Margo said, remembering the car ride and the black teenagers, "I can't guarantee that. But I can guarantee I'll speak to him about it if he does."

"You'll have to be very nice to me after this," Rae said, forcing the corners of her mouth up almost into a smile. "You owe me. Just wait till I bring my mother here."

Her father was still standing, unsure of the choice of seats. There was the futon, which was too low, and a purple stool at Rae's drafting table, which was too high, and an old armchair covered with two sleeping cats. Rae surprised the cats when she pushed them to the floor saying, "Have a seat, Mr. Kresko."

Margo brought in the drinks and some raw vegetables and hummus she'd prepared the night before. "Rae's gonna stay home while we go out," Margo said, offering the hummus, which her father declined. "She has to work." When her father didn't question that, Margo went on proudly, "Rae's illustrating a children's book that a friend of hers wrote. They have an agent who's trying to place it somewhere."

Margo's father smiled and nodded and continued to examine every inch of the apartment with his eyes. Finally, they came to rest on the flat futon on the floor in the adjoining room, visible through the open French doors.

"Nice doors, huh, Dad?" Margo said, to deflect his interest in the bedroom. "Bet you haven't seen doors like that in a while.

"My mother's house had them, on Metropolitan Street,"

he smiled. "That house was built in the twenties, about when I was born."

"This building, too," Rae noted. "You can tell from the fixtures."

"Rae knows a lot about architecture," Margo said, for no particular reason except to fill in the silence.

"You don't have much room," her father pointed out, his eyes still wandering back to the bedroom. "Maybe I should stay at a hotel, like your mother and I did last time." At the words "your mother," his voice wavered momentarily.

"Don't be silly, there's plenty of room," Margo objected. "You're better off here with us."

Her father finished his Tab but didn't try the hummus, saying politely that he wasn't hungry, but probably thinking, Margo decided, that it was a funny color for food.

...

On the deck of the Intrepid, Margo and her father leaned against the railing and looked into the motionless water below, instead of at each other.

"It would be better," her father said, "if they'd let you go into the crew's quarters. That's the real interesting part."

"Maybe next time you come that section will be open," Margo offered, helpfully.

"Well, this isn't the World War II Intrepid anyway," he sighed, disappointment in his voice. They had discovered once on board that the ship was a later Intrepid, one built after the war. Margo wasn't sure if he was disappointed with the boat, with her for bringing him there, or with time in general. "This isn't as big as the carriers we had during the war. You should have seen them, they were really something."

Margo turned and leaned her elbows on the railing, catching the sad look in his eyes as she did. He was still staring off into the water, his hands folded tightly on top of the railing, his body looking thinner and more frail than usual. His sporty clothes—one of many outfits he had bought in the last few years—hung on him loosely. She remembered teasing them both, on one of her trips home, about the clothes they had accumulated in their retirement. Margo had not been able to find a single empty clothes hanger in the closet that had been hers and Dottie's, because it was filled to overflowing with her mother's new dresses and pant suits. She went into her brother's old room, and the closet in there held an array of colorful sport jackets and casual pants. Laughing, she asked what was in the closet in *their* bedroom. "Oh, that got filled up a long time ago," her father smiled. He had rummaged through it for a hanger for her.

"Where do you wear all these clothes?" Margo had asked, as she hung up the one shirt she didn't want to wrinkle.

"Oh, when we go to plays or out to dinner. We belong to the Retirees Club at church, you know, and we go on day trips with them," her father had answered. "They have dances and things, too." Margo smiled at the memory of them when she was younger, her father always in his blue denim work clothes, her mother in one of two cotton print housedresses. Only on Saturday nights had they taken out their "good" clothes for their weekly dinner and dancing date.

"Boy," Margo had said, finding an empty space for her shirt, "you guys get out more than I do."

Now she was so startled by her father's fragile profile that she blurted out, "You look a little thin, Dad. Are you eating okay?"

"Fine," he said, a little too quickly.

"You make yourself dinner?" she pursued.

"Your sister taught me to cook a few things," he smiled,

not really answering the question. "Spaghetti, meatloaf, and stuffed peppers. They're not like your mother's, though," he added quietly.

"Does Dottie invite you to dinner sometimes?" she continued. Margo felt a little guilty that watching out for their widowed father had fallen to Dottie, the only one of the three kids who lived nearby. Jack had lived in California for years and rarely came home. Conveniently, Dottie and her husband Carl lived just five minutes from her father.

"Oh, yeah," her father said emphatically. "Carl and her are real good about that. I go there a couple of times a week at least."

They were still talking about nothing, Margo thought. Food, drink, warships, French doors. She wanted to say to him, How do you *feel*, but her family never talked about anything as dangerous as feelings. Then, seemingly out of nowhere, but probably because it was always on his mind, Margo's father said, "I miss your mother," without any prompting from his daughter.

And she replied, just as naturally, "Me too."

After the Intrepid they faced each other in a restaurant Margo had chosen for its broad American menu. Her father was pleased and picked a basic steak and baked potato dinner.

"You know," Margo said, "I was just thinking about your record collection last week. Some guy on the street was selling 78's like yours for ten bucks each."

"They're worth more than that, in good condition," he corrected.

"Oh," she said, disappointed that she hadn't told him something new.

"Besides, I gave mine away," he added. "To Marty Ranicki."

"Your 78's? Daddy, you loved those records," Margo

said, a sudden sadness and nostalgia welling up in her throat. "You took such good care of them, how could you give them away? Who's this Marty Ranicki anyway, I never heard of him."

"Sure, you did," he insisted. "I talked about Marty all the time. From the Army. We were on Guam together. He's the one we called Moe."

"Oh," Margo said, "yeah, Moe."

"What good were they doing me anyhow? Just a bunch of old records I bought when I was a kid." Her father finished half his dinner and pushed it toward her, covering it with his napkin for emphasis. "I hadn't listened to them for months, since your mother got sick."

Margo ate half her dinner, too, but left it uncovered because her father was staring at it so intently, seemingly mesmerized by the pattern of uneaten carrots and green beans on the side of the plate.

"You should eat your vegetables," he said, finally.

"So should you," she smiled.

...

In the car again heading back to the apartment, Margo asked her father to stop at a little bar they passed on the Lower East Side.

"You'll love this place, Dad," she said, as they sat down at one of the wobbly tables in the back. "The jukebox plays mostly Glenn Miller and Frank Sinatra. I always think of you when I come here."

Her father looked confused. He hadn't been in a bar, he said, since the war.

"Well, this one hasn't changed a whole lot since then," she smiled.

They didn't have diet soda, so she got him a club soda and herself a draft beer. The bartender gave her quarters for the jukebox, which was playing someone else's selection, and her finger purposely skipped over "Strangers in the Night," in favor of some older songs.

Well into her first beer, Margo decided to take the risk and ask how he liked Rae.

"She seems nice," he said.

"Yeah, she is," Margo agreed.

"I don't know what your mother would say, though," he added.

"About what?"

"About a colored girl," he said, after hesitating.

Margo took a deep breath, afraid to say anything for fear of setting off a fight, but knowing that she had to.

"Look, Dad, Rae is a black woman. It's offensive to me to hear you say 'colored.' And she's a grown woman, not a girl."

To her amazement, he didn't argue. It had been a long day. "All right," he said, wearily, "a *black woman*. I don't know what your mother would say about a *black woman*." The emphasis held a hint of sarcasm, but at least, she thought, he said the words. Then he laughed. "Well, she was never crazy about the *woman* part, so I guess the color wouldn't make a difference." He hesitated and strummed his fingers nervously on the table, in perfect time to "String of Pearls." "Oh, I don't know. I know she got upset about you. But if she was here," he said, tapping the table with his index finger, "if she was here, I'd tell her the only thing worth getting upset about is somebody dying."

He turned his face away, furtively wiping his eyes. When she asked if he wanted to go, he said he was enjoying the music. He misses his records, she realized. They stayed for a second round, waiting for Margo's selections to come up on the jukebox. But instead, unmistakably, she heard the opening bars of "Strangers in the Night," and her throat went dry. She wondered suddenly if she'd brought him here just to hear it. His expression didn't change; he still looked sad. He watched the other customers, tapping his fingers again, but not in time to the song. She thought she saw a few beads of sweat above his lip.

Margo stood up, put her hand over his on the table. "Wanna dance?" she asked, and for a moment he looked like he would refuse to be made a spectacle. But then he stood up, too, and took her hand without a word, and they danced in the narrow space between the bar and the tables.

CYSTERS

Rebecca rolled from one side to the other, trying to find a comfortable position. She couldn't stay on her right side because of the pain, but if she lay on her left side for too long her arm started to feel numb. If she slept on her back or stomach all night, she knew she would wake up with a backache. So she rolled back onto the right and contemplated the pain she thought she felt.

She couldn't tell if it was really pain. It was more of an intense discomfort, like someone had put a weight on her internal organs. That, she thought, must be the cyst. Or was it just her imagination? She wanted it to be just the product of creative hypochondria, but she suspected that wasn't the case.

Eight months before, she'd been diagnosed with a right ovarian cyst the size of an orange. Now every time she thought about it, it was a dimpled orange ball growing from her fallopian tube like from a vine. She preferred not to think about it, had spent four months judiciously avoiding it. The first four months had been filled with doctors' opinions, sonograms and the completion of dozens of medical insurance forms. All of it had been more painful than the cyst.

"I want you to get your life in order," the first doctor told her. "I don't want to waste any more time getting you into the hospital."

"The hospital?" Rebecca asked, shrinking a little in her chair.

"The best thing is surgery, just get rid of it. I won't kid you. This is major surgery: a week in the hospital, four to six weeks recovery. That's why you need to get your life in order." The doctor had flipped over the pages of a spiral standing notebook facing Rebecca, showing in full color all the things that could possibly go wrong with a woman's reproductive system. Each one was worse than the last.

Why do I have to deal with this? Rebecca thought, while the doctor explained about different kinds of cysts.

"I was hoping yours would be the fluid type and that there would be a chance that it would go away on its own. Unfortunately, that's not the case." The doctor closed the notebook. "Do you have any questions? I know this is a lot to take in right now."

"How soon does this surgery have to happen?" Rebecca asked weakly.

"I'd like you to be admitted within the next two weeks. We shouldn't wait longer than that."

"Why?" Rebecca asked, searching for the words that she couldn't believe she would say in a sentence about herself. "Is it cancerous?"

"No, no, that's highly unlikely in a woman your age. You're thirty, aren't you?"

"Thirty-two."

"No, hardly ever with a woman that young," the doctor repeated. "If you were forty-five, fifty, there would be a greater chance of cancer. Of course, we can never really tell until we're inside there."

"So what's the danger?" Rebecca repeated.

"Rupture," the doctor said, flipping the notebook open again to a graphic illustration of a brown mass exploding all over a woman's pretty pink organs. It looked like something from a comic book—"The Cyst That Ate New

York." Rebecca turned her eyes away quickly. "That could happen at any time," the doctor said, leaving the notebook open to that page and leaning back in her chair thoughtfully. "Also, there's the pain."

"The pain?" Rebecca asked, startled. She had said repeatedly that she hadn't had any pain for months, not since the first time that sent her to the doctor with what she thought was an ulcer. "What pain?"

"You must be in pain, with a cyst of that size," the doctor insisted, with a piercing look, as if, Rebecca thought, she were willing her to have pain. "Of course, the other danger is that you won't be able to conceive."

"I'm not planning on having children," Rebecca said.

"Well, if you change your mind, you would definitely want that cyst out." The doctor leaned forward again and took a business card from her desk. "I want you to call me within the week so we can schedule an admitting date for the hospital."

Rebecca had gotten up numbly, controlling the explosion of tears that was backed up inside her. She paid eighty dollars at the front desk for her ten-minute consultation, walked into the street and around the corner before she let herself cry. She cried all the way home on the subway, and the fact that no one gave her a second look made her cry even harder.

She found herself worrying constantly about rupture and its ugly consequences. She was afraid to do anything strenuous, like lifting or running, for fear of falling onto the ground in a heap.

"What happened to her?" some New Yorker would ask.

"Looks like a rupture," another would answer.

And who would they call? She still carried in her wallet a scrap of paper that read, "In case of emergency call Brenda Nardozzi," with two phone numbers where they wouldn't reach Brenda anymore. And who would she call, if she had to go to the hospital in the middle of the night? She hated to bother her friends, her family was five hundred miles away, and Brenda had moved to Boston with her new lover. Rebecca decided she would just dial 911 and hope that it really worked the way they said it would.

The second doctor allayed her fears a little. Without openly criticizing the first doctor, he said that worrying about rupture was doing her no good. He was in less of a hurry to admit her to the hospital.

"What kind of birth control do you use?" he asked, scribbling her name across a medical form.

"I don't," Rebecca said. "I'm a lesbian."

He looked at her without changing expressions, though the honesty of her answer had made him hesitate. His pen was poised for writing "diaphragm" or "pill" and he thought carefully before jotting "lesbian" into the blank space. He proceeded with the questions and filled up one side of the form.

"I'd like to start you on birth control pills, which will sometimes reduce the cyst," he said, and Rebecca's stomach sank. She had never used birth control and had become a little smug about not having to. When her straight friends complained about the mess or the inconvenience of birth control, she came back with, "There's always the sure-fire method—switch to women!"

For her third opinion she went to a homeopath, even though she wasn't sure she believed in the principles of it. She came right out and told him she was skeptical.

"I think it's all just little sugar pills," Rebecca explained, "and it's based on the principle that if you *believe* you're getting better, then you will."

The homeopath wrote that down. He also wrote down everything she said for the next hour. At the end, she was exhausted from all his questions. She was also a little embarrassed. Questions as varied as "How often do you belch?" and "How is your sex drive?" made her feel like giggling, like a kid instead of a thirty-two-year-old. Mature adults should be able to say "flatulance" without snickering, but the whole thing just seemed so silly.

It did, however, bring some things into perspective very quickly. His questions got right to the heart of everything that was making her sad, and thus possibly ill—much more quickly than the painstaking, week after week ordeal of psychotherapy.

"Six months ago my lover announced it was 'time' for us to break up, for no apparent reason," Rebecca explained, glad to get the story off her chest one more time. "She thought it was better to break up while we were still getting along. It turned out she was interested in a woman she worked with. They became lovers while we were still going out, and now they've moved to Boston together." At the same time, she found herself dealing with a new and more difficult job and a move from the apartment she'd shared with Brenda.

"You've had a lot of upheaval in a short time," the homeopath remarked. "I'm surprised the cyst isn't the size of a basketball."

He described ovarian cysts as the "woman's ulcer," the specific way that a woman's body reacts to intense stress. "You're not alone. This is becoming more and more common. I've treated more women for cysts in the last five years than I could count." This was some small comfort to Rebecca, at least to know she had lots of company. Cysters, she thought, but it was only briefly amusing.

The best thing about the homeopath was that he said exactly what she wanted to hear. "You don't need surgery for an ovarian cyst," were the magic words that brought her back to him several times. Each time he changed her sugar pills slightly or gave her a Bach flower remedy or asked again how her sex drive was. She wanted to believe that the cyst was shrinking into a little brown raisin that would completely wither and disappear. She stopped drinking coffee, ate more vegetables, took her pills religiously. Her friends were encouraging, told her they believed it was going away. She almost did, too, but it was hard not knowing what was going on inside her body. The homeopath gave her something for "anxiety about the unknown." But when two of her friends were also diagnosed with right ovarian cysts, Rebecca, losing hope and confidence, stopped taking her sugar pills.

Now on her right side, she thought she could feel it. She pressed on her lower abdomen to see if there was pain or a lump, but there wasn't. Had it grown, like her friend Alice's, to cover both sides, not just the right? Was it spreading across her vital organs? Had it become cancerous through neglect? Was it too late to try birth control pills? It seemed ironic that cysts grew from unfertilized eggs, something that could have been life itself becoming a threat of death. A punishment, some religious conservatives might say, for not having babies like women were supposed to.

Rebecca got up for two aspirin and lay back down carefully. She had been lying there, thinking, thinking, thinking, for two hours, and exhaustion came over her suddenly. She probably would not have to go to the hospital tonight, she reasoned with herself, and she could arrange a fourth opinion in the morning. She tried her best to think of nothing, she patted her own head, she felt one tear slide over the bridge of her nose to the pillow.

Like Mother, Like. . .

When Emma got off the plane at Newark Airport, her mother wasn't there. She always half-expected her to be standing there, smiling and waving and greeting her like other people were greeting the other passengers. So she was always a little disappointed, even though it was not the kind of thing her mother would do or, in fact, even think of. "You're coming in Friday night?" her mother had said on the phone the other day and almost every time Emma came to town. "Great, honey. I'm going out, but I'll see you late that night or early Saturday." It was usually Saturday, as Emma remembered.

It was a short flight from Boston, and an inexpensive one, and Emma usually came to New York every other month. She stayed at her mother's apartment, the one on West 16th Street where they'd lived ever since Emma was little. She saw her friends from Barnard and went shopping and to see a play or to AREA on Saturday night. On Sunday afternoon, if her mother wasn't too busy, they might go out for a leisurely brunch and talk about Emma's job at the bank, her mother's graduate classes at Columbia, what books they'd read and other general chitchat. On these occasions, Emma sometimes found herself wondering why she'd moved to Boston, but she always went back on Sunday night.

She found a note from her mother when she reached the

apartment. "Gone to a forum on Women in Nicaragua. Started at 8, if you get in in time. P.S. 41. If not, see you later. Love, Jessica." She had called her mother "Jessica" for the past ten years or more, but had never really gotten used to seeing it in print. Love, Jessica. Jessica, she knew, would love it if she showed up at P.S. 41 for a political forum. It was only eight-thirty and the school was close by. But she would have rather gone out for dinner. If Ben, her boyfriend, had been with her, they would have done just that. She wished the note from Jessica had said, "Meet us at the Odeon." Emma put it down and went into the bathroom to wash her face. She changed from her business suit into jeans and a sweater and settled down on her mother's bed to make some phone calls.

She was annoyed when Alison's answering machine answered instead of Alison. They had made tentative plans to go out. Emma hung up after leaving a slightly curt message and tried Suzanne next. Her roommate said she'd gone to Boston for the weekend. "Would you like her to call you on Monday?"

"Only if she'll still be in Boston," Emma said, explaining that she was just in for the weekend. She tried calling a few more friends whom she hadn't told she was coming into town, but they were all out already enjoying the weekend. Emma pulled on her blazer and went out into the street.

It was almost nine-thirty when she strolled past P.S. 41, licking an ice cream cone from Steve's. There was a crowd of women on the street in front of the school, spilling out of the doors, their many conversations becoming one, indistinguishable buzz. She stood to the right of the doors, looking for a face she recognized. Pretty soon she was in a sea of women in blue jeans wearing buttons that said "U.S. Out of Central America" and "No More Vietnams." They were so many types of the same person, she thought—thin, fat, tall, short, white, black, all obviously agitated by whatever had gone on inside. Emma stood watching them, a little afraid that they would sweep her away in their enthusiasm. When she heard, "Jessica, look who I found," she turned gratefully toward the woman who'd put her hand on her shoulder.

"Emma, it's so good to see you again," said the woman, who enveloped Emma in her green trenchcoat. Emma was not sure she would have recognized Laura, her mother's lover, from the last time she'd seen her if she hadn't come up to her first. They had, after all, only had coffee together one morning two months before, and Laura's hair had gotten considerably shorter. It had been shoulder length then, but was now only an inch long all over her head.

"Hi, Laura, how are you?" she asked, politely kissing her on the cheek. "Where's my mother?"

"She was right behind me, but in this crowd. . . " Laura turned and caught Jessica by the hand. "Here she is. This is some crowd, isn't it?"

Jessica hugged Emma tightly. "Honey, you look great. I'm glad you decided to meet us here." She took a bite of the cone. "Cookies and Cream, my favorite," she said, winking at Laura.

Jessica was stunning as always, not beautiful in a conventional way, but bright and dynamic and spontaneous. She always exuded a kind of contagious energy, and her hair and clothes looked as if she'd just run in from somewhere. She took Emma's breath away a little, both literally and figuratively, walking down the street as quickly as she went through her life. Jessica had never had enough time to do everything she wanted to, but she tried very hard. She had managed to cram a lot of events and friends and jobs into the last twenty years that Emma remembered.

"I'm sorry you missed the forum," Jessica said, putting one arm through Laura's and the other through Emma's as they headed toward Sixth Avenue. "It was phenonmenal.

Presentations by women who recently came back from Nicaragua, with poetry and slides and music. It was really inspiring. Didn't you love it?" she asked, turning toward Laura for confirmation.

Laura nodded less than enthusiastically. "It was well done, but I guess I'm feeling a little inundated with the Women in Central America theme."

"Well, I feel that way sometimes, too, but this was just so moving. Especially the poems. I wanted to go there myself." Jessica turned again toward Emma. "They were beautiful, written by women who'd actually fought in the revolution. You know, it's a whole country of poets practically. That kind of thing really gets to me." Emma smiled weakly and squeezed her mother's arm. "When did you get in, honey?" Jessica continued. "I can't get over how great you look. Doesn't she look great, Laura? I like that haircut a lot. Shorter hair looks better on you, I think, it makes your face look fuller. And speaking of haircuts, what do you think of this crewcut?" she asked, running a hand playfully over Laura's head. "I couldn't believe she did it. Took me a week to get used to it. It's grown out now, you should've seen it two weeks ago."

"I finally tried the Astor Place barbershop," Laura explained. "I think they overdid it a little, but it does feel pretty good. I feel totally butch," she added, putting an arm around Jessica's shoulder. Laura was a tall woman who towered over both Emma and her mother. She was considerably younger than Jessica, probably by about ten or twelve years, but she already had traces of grey in her hair that made her seem the older of the two.

"Where do you want to go?" Jessica asked. "How about Moreno's?"

Emma said that would be fine, and it was one of the few things she'd said since Laura came up to her in front of the school. It was always that way with Mother and her friends

and lovers: they were always coming out of a political meeting or a foreign film or some new lesbian play that made
them totally excited and overly talkative. Emma was often
included in the plans, Jessica hoping that her daughter
would catch the same enthusiasm for political life that she
had had as a young antiwar activist and then as a feminist in
the women's movement. She had surrounded her daughter
with "good people," a seemingly endless string of long-
haired, guitar-playing men and women when she was little,
and then, when she was an adolescent, of short-haired,
guitar-playing women. Emma could chronicle her mother's
political transformations through the events of her own life,
the fact that at some point they had stopped eating ham-
burgers and chicken and ate more vegetables and tofu; the
fact that her mother began taking her to Holly Near con-
certs instead of Peter, Paul, and Mary; the fact that there
was first her father and then a lot of men and then almost no
men at all in their lives. She was the only girl she knew who
had been named for a political figure, Emma Goldman, and
who had cats named Sappho and Colette. How many times
had she wished for her friend Alison's mother, who wore
dresses instead of jeans, even in the house, gave elegant dinner parties for her husband's business clients, and most im-
portantly, acted her age. Jessica had always seemed to be
about twenty, as far as Emma could see. Emma had been
shocked by Jessica's fortieth birthday four years before,
more surprised and incredulous about it than her mother. "I
feel great," Jessica had said, and Emma had to admit, she
looked it. But she was more a companion than what Emma
imagined a mother was, the kind who stayed home, like on
television, and cooked and baked and worried about the
shine on the floor. It was appropriate that she had almost
never called her Mother, except sometimes out of exaspera-
tion. "Mother, pu-lease," had been a familiar phrase of her
late adolescence, but it had been replaced by "Oh, really,

Jessica," after Emma went to college.

"I don't know why I like this place," Jessica was saying, when they'd found a table at Moreno's. "I've been coming here for years, too. Something about it is like San Francisco and your father," she said to Emma, who didn't remember San Francisco, hardly knew her father and didn't like the restaurant.

Emma had been born in San Francisco when her father was in graduate school at Stanford, and they had lived there for about four years before coming back to New York, where both of her parents had grown up. Her father had stayed in California, and she had seen him so infrequently since then that he was little more to her than a face in some photographs of her mother's. "We got married too young," Jessica had explained when Emma had asked why she didn't have a live-in father like Alison. "We didn't know each other very well, didn't know what we wanted. The only good thing that came out of those five years was you—and my independence."

The waitress checked at their table several times to see if they were ready to order, but each time Emma ruffled the pages of her menu and said, a little frantically, "Another minute, please." Jessica and Laura had already ordered their food and two draft beers. When the waitress brought the drinks, Emma closed her menu in a defeated way and said simply, "I'll take a Heineken." She drank beer rarely, preferring gin martinis with a twist, and she almost never ate in coffee shop-like places with menus that went on and on for pages, mostly, she suspected, to hide the fact that the food they served wasn't very good.

"Not hungry?" Jessica asked, but she had never been the kind of mother who worried if her child didn't eat, especially after Emma reached the age of ten or eleven. "Emma won't let herself starve," Jessica had pointed out, when a relative had noticed that teenaged Emma was rushing out to a dance with friends instead of finishing dinner. She was also not the kind of mother who would say, "You're looking thin" or "You're looking fat"; it just would never have occurred to her that it was her business to comment on it.

So the "Not hungry?" was all she said, and then she started talking about her new Women and Fiction class and how the professor had been too ambitious in her course plan. "Of course, there's hardly anything by Third World women to speak of, just a few thrown in here and there. And not much mention of the part lesbians played in creating fiction. I guess I'd just like it acknowledged that Willa Cather was a lesbian, you know what I mean?"

Emma nodded reluctantly; she was not really sure what Jessica *did* mean, but Laura seemed to. Laura was watching Jessica's mouth for every word that came out of it, in such an obviously advanced state of love that Emma felt a little embarrassed. She was not sure why, except that on top of everything—the fact that Jessica didn't cook or bake or wear dresses or have a husband or act forty-four—she was a lesbian, too. Emma had gotten used to it, had, in fact, lived with it for over ten years, but it still wasn't something she understood. Emma, for example, thought Laura was an attractive woman, but she couldn't imagine wanting to go to bed with her. What was it that brought two women together like a woman and a man? Jessica had never tried to proselytize and had been very careful not to sway Emma's ideas about sexuality. Emma was eleven when her mother came out to her. "Karen, the woman who stayed over here last night? She's someone I'm very fond of, and I'm going to be seeing a lot of her. She'll be around the house." A long pause. A nervous twitch of Jessica's eye. "Do you know what the word 'homosexual' means?"

Emma had said that some kids used the words "homo" and "faggot" at school to mock out the sissy boys.

"Well, you should never do that, because it's not a bad

thing to be a homosexual. It's just different from what most people are used to. And you shouldn't call people 'queer' either."

"Why not?" Emma asked, watching the little beads of perspiration appearing on her mother's forehead.

"It's like 'nigger,' it's offensive, it puts people down who haven't hurt you," Jessica answered in a defensive tone, rubbing the back of her hand over her forehead. Another long pause. "I have to tell you this, because I want you to hear it from me, not at school or in the street. I'm... "

Emma had felt her heart race, not making the connection between the last few minutes of conversation and what Jessica was trying to say. For a moment she was convinced Jessica was dying.

"... a homosexual, a lesbian. I don't expect you to understand right now, and I know I'm botching this up, but if I ever hear you say 'queer' or 'dyke,' I'll... I'll... oh, I don't know what I'll do."

Jessica had left the room, flushed and shaking. Later that day and on several more occasions when she was calmer, Jessica had tried to explain things better, using funny words like "woman-identified." Emma had been totally confused for a long time, and had wondered if she, too, would become a lesbian because her mother was one and didn't used to be. Emma remembered when her mother had had several boyfriends at one time. Maybe Emma would become "queer," too, later on, unless there was something she could do to prevent it.

She worried when, at twelve, she had fooled around with James Lyle after school and he had put his tongue into her mouth. "What are you *doing*?" she asked in horror, sure that she would get some terrible disease from having a strange tongue inside her mouth. Maybe that was a sign, she thought, the first indication that the old saying was right: Like mother, like daughter. After worrying about it for days, during which she avoided James and most of her other friends, she finally blurted out her fear to her mother. Jessica smiled and put her arm around her. "But lesbians do that to each other, too, honey. Do you think it was James you didn't like, or just the tongue, or boys in general? What if Alison or one of your girlfriends had done that to you?"

Emma had to admit that she didn't think she would have liked that any better, that in fact kissing James at first had been sort of nice, until he'd opened up his mouth. "I think my being a lesbian confuses you about yourself, but it doesn't have anything to do with you. You'll make your own decisions when you're ready."

At eighteen, her first semester at Barnard, Emma had decided to sleep with Michael and then decided to keep doing that for a while. Over the next few years, she decided on other boys whom she liked or loved in varying degrees. She never decided on any women. Her senior year, she became engaged to a law student, whom she'd been dating for about a year. But it broke off when he started talking about a baby within the first year of marriage. She'd moved to Boston after graduation, where she'd gotten the best job offer, and spent some time alone before starting to see Ben, the man she was still involved with. Ben worked as a loan officer at the bank where she was in international marketing. They hadn't talked about marriage—she thought twenty-three was still too young—but he was the kind of man she thought she could be with for a long time. They had similar goals. They both wanted careers in banking and money to do all the things they liked. They both wanted a Victorian house with antiques and a sailboat and a summer place on the Cape. Ben was ambitious, something Emma admired a lot, and he'd moved up at the bank quickly since he'd started there five years before, just out of Harvard Business School. He was a little more conservative than Emma was used to, but not old-fashioned in his view of women. He always told her he admired her determination to have a career and thought she would probably be an AVP at the bank within a short time.

Emma had not brought him home to meet her mother yet; it was something she thought she should work up to. She had told her mother all about him one day over brunch, and Jessica had asked a lot of polite questions without making comment on the answers. Jessica always inquired about him on Emma's subsequent visits home and said she'd like to meet him. But Emma had overheard a conversation between Jessica and Laura the last time she'd been in New York, when they were sitting over coffee in the kitchen and didn't know she was up yet.

"She told me he voted for Reagan, and that that bothered her," Jessica said.

"Well, at least that's something," Laura replied. "At least *she* didn't vote for him. At least it bothered her."

"I know, but how many times have you heard of people in love affecting each other's opinions? We do it with each other in little ways all the time. And she's gotten to be so materialistic since college. When I ask how she is, she tells me what she's bought recently. She had a really liberal upbringing, but sometimes I think she wants to rebel against it, that all along she hated the way I dealt with her." There was a crack in Jessica's voice. "Well, it *is* my doing. I brought her up to be her own person, and here she is. I guess there's no guarantee your kids will want to be like you. I just always thought my way was the best, such a clear choice, that she'd naturally grow up to be a liberal, maybe even a lesbian. But when you think about it, I certainly didn't want to turn out like my mother." Jessica had sighed heavy-heartedly. "Sometimes I feel so stupid, like I should say to myself, she's my daughter and I love her and she's a good person and who cares if she's turned into a heterosexual yuppie. God, sometimes I wish I weren't so political, that it didn't really matter to me."

It was one of the first glimpses she'd really had of her mother, that there was disappointment on both sides of their relationship, and it made her angry. It was all right for her to wish for Alison's mother, but the idea that Jessica had probably wondered, "Why can't Emma be like Alice Rosen's daughter Terra, who does solidarity work? Or Eva Kincaid's Lisa, who's living with her lover at the women's peace camp?" seemed like a betrayal. Her mother, she had always thought, accepted her unconditionally, but now here she was, complaining to someone who didn't even know Emma. Emma had gone back to Boston early, in quiet defiance, but had gotten over her anger in the next few days. She realized that she, too, had wondered how they could be mother and daughter, with their different values and world views. Sitting at the table in Moreno's, across from her mother and her lesbian lover, Emma wondered where on earth she had come from.

They finished their order and Emma picked up the bill to pay for it. "I just got a raise, I forgot to tell you," she explained. "My treat." But she had not forgotten to tell her, Emma had just thought Jessica would take in the information in about the same way she would "I missed the bus today" or "Ben bought a new suit." She was right: both Jessica and Laura thanked her and said congratulations, before moving on to the next topic. Ben had taken her out to dinner to celebrate, to an expensive dinner for fresh lobster. She would never dream of telling Jessica that. Jessica didn't eat lobster and thought it practically criminal to do so. "I can't get past the way they kill them," she'd say. It would only make the disappointment more acute: she wouldn't lecture Emma, just talk about it with Laura that night in bed or the next morning over coffee.

They walked home at Jessica's usual clip, Laura entertaining them with stories of characters she'd run into in the Village. She was very amusing and Emma found herself feeling fond of her. To Emma's surprise, they dropped Laura off at her apartment on West 10th before continuing on home.

"I thought she'd stay over," Emma commented, when they were on their way again.

"Oh, we see each other all the time," Jessica said. "We talked about living together, but neither of us wants to give up our apartment! Anyway, Laura has to get up early to go to a conference tomorrow."

"You're not going?" Emma asked incredulously. She had never known her mother to miss a conference on purpose, and she was sure if it interested Laura, it would interest Jessica, too.

"No," Jessica said. "I have to work on an article about the forum tonight for the feminist newspaper. It's due Sunday, and I promised. What are your plans?"

Emma's heart sank to her stomach. For a minute, she had imagined that her mother was giving up the conference to be with her and had planned an afternoon of shopping and cocktails.

"I tried to reach Alison," Emma said, trying not to sound disappointed, "but she wasn't home. I guess I'll try again tomorrow. I don't have any definite plans."

After a pause, Jessica said, "Maybe I can finish the article early and we can have brunch."

Emma brightened. "If it's no problem, maybe we could."

"I'll give it my best shot," Jessica smiled.

They reached the apartment, and Jessica went first to the answering machine. There were a few miscellaneous messages, including one from Alison, and a "Goodnight, I love you" one from Laura. "I think I'll go call her, then try to do a little reading for class. Your old mother's out of the swing of this homework stuff. I never thought going back to graduate school full time would be so hard to adjust to. It's even more tiring than working and taking a class at night, I think." Jessica smiled and kissed her on the cheek. "Goodnight, honey. Nice to have you home again."

Emma started into her old bedroom, but heard Jessica calling her before she'd reached it. "Oh, Emma, I forgot. You need sheets on the bed. You know where they are, right? Goodnight, honey."

Emma grabbed some sheets and a blanket out of the linen closet on her way to the bedroom. She switched on the light and looked at the bare twin bed in front of her. It was just another thing Jessica would never do, for whatever reason. She shrugged, made the bed, and decided to wait until Jessica was off the phone so she could call Ben.

A Matter of Convenience

Jo propped herself up on one elbow to get a better look at Diane, who was sleeping soundly with just the faintest sliver of moonlight across her face. She was more attractive than Jo had noticed before, especially pretty and vulnerable in sleep, one of her breasts edging out over the top of the sheet. Jo's head throbbed a little from the frozen daiquiris they'd whipped up in Diane's blender that evening, after buying some of each kind of fruit at the corner green grocer. By the time they got to making the kiwi banana ones, they couldn't remember what flavor they'd started with. Diane seemed to be all hands, running them over Jo's breasts, her thighs, her ass. They had ended up on the living room floor having what Diane had been known to describe as "tooth-rattling sex." How they got to bed Jo couldn't remember. But the clock now said 3 A.M. and the pain in her head was matched only by the throbbing in her back from sleeping double in a too soft single bed. Jo tried to shift without waking Diane, but after several tries had only moved an inch or two. Diane smiled in her sleep, maybe dreaming about their escapades on the floor. Diane liked sex more than Jo did. Or she liked sex with Jo more than Jo liked it with Diane. Watching the dreamy smile part Diane's lips, Jo thought, what am I doing here?

Suddenly, a panic rose in her, a feeling of physical confinement, of being pushed up against a wall and not being allowed to move. She nudged Diane a little, hoping she'd move away toward the edge of the bed, but she only sighed in her sleep and moved closer to snuggle. The pain in Jo's back from lying too long in the same position seemed unbearable. Jo felt her throat getting tight, the tightness starting in her chest and traveling up, up to her throat till it was so pronounced she couldn't swallow it back. She sat up, but Diane didn't budge. How could she sleep? Alcohol kept Jo awake or woke her from sleep at odd hours and then kept her too restless and anxious to fall back asleep. She coughed, and Diane only mumbled something and closed her lips. Jo felt herself starting to cry, knew she would burst into tears if she didn't get up and move around. Maybe I'll get some water, she thought, and even crawling over Diane didn't faze her. It was the shrieking of the cat, which Jo stepped on by the side of the bed, that finally roused Diane.

"Honey, are you okay?" she asked. It was amazing to Jo how someone could wake up suddenly and in the next minute be attentive to another person's needs.

"I'm fine, just thirsty." Jo went into the living room naked, the coolness of the night air refreshing her after the closeness of the bed. She realized when she got to the bathroom that she didn't know where the light switch was, that even though she'd stayed over a half-dozen times, she was still a stranger in the apartment. Diane, she thought, probably always turned the light on for her. She left the door open for the shaft of light that cut across the living room, splashed water on her face, and cupped some in her hands to drink.

"The glasses are all in the kitchen," Diane said, when Jo got back to the room, as if she could anticipate Jo's every need. She was sitting up with the nightstand lamp on. "Sorry, I should've warned you."

"It's okay, Diane, really," Jo said, realizing that she

hardly ever said Diane's name. It sounded strange using it now. "You apologize too much."

Diane smiled, looking confused, then held out her hand. "C'mere," she said.

"It's so hot in here," Jo said, taking her time coming back to the bed. "It's nice and cool in the living room. Maybe we should leave the door open."

"Not a good idea," Diane grinned. "I heard Peg come in after we'd moved in here. She's already complained about how much noise we make. "

Jo crawled back over her to her eighteen inches of mattress. "Really?" she asked, blushing. "We should watch that."

"Look, I told her I pay half the rent and that she has to realize that people have sex. I didn't say it, but I think she's just mad because she hasn't been laid in a year. I don't think we should restrain ourselves for *her*."

"I guess it's a little annoying, though, if you want to have sex but aren't," Jo offered, feeling sympathetic to Peg. She herself had gone through long periods of celibacy after difficult breakups. Once, on a camping trip with a group of friends, Jo had been woken in the middle of the night to one woman's moans of ecstacy. She had lain there, alone in her sleeping bag, heart pounding, head sweating, mind racing. Instead of trying to go back to sleep or plugging her ears, she'd lain there motionless, wondering who was doing what to whom, and remembering the pleasure of sex in a tent in the Catskills with her lover Katherine, who had since left her. When the woman finally came, there were tears in the corners of Jo's eyes and a hollowness in her chest that she hadn't felt since the breakup with Kate.

"So let her get a girlfriend," Diane snapped. She pulled up close to Jo, who was lying on her back, and began licking her left ear. When she blew into it hotly, Jo shivered, but not the way Diane intended.

"I don't feel like it," Jo said, propping her head up on her arms so that she was out of range of Diane's tongue.

"That's a new one," Diane said, looking stunned by her failure. They had been dating for eight weeks, having frequent sex, drinking champagne in bed and having intimate candlelit dinners at home, and, in general, having what was by many people's standards a very romantic affair. Till now, Diane had never failed at seducing Jo.

"We don't have to have sex every moment we're awake," Jo said, crisply. "I mean, we never *talk*, we just drink and eat and have sex." Jo felt the pain in her head spreading, filling her skull till she thought it would crack. "Do you have any aspirin?"

Diane nodded, said "I'll get it," and jumped up before Jo could protest. Shouldn't she appreciate a woman who waited on her—brought her breakfast in bed, always made the dinner and theater reservations, gave long backrubs instead of two-minute ones and never expected Jo to reciprocate? But Jo never knew exactly what to *say* to Diane. Diane was an intelligent woman, a successful management consultant, but they always seemed to be just bumping against each other's thoughts and then veering off in the other direction.

Jo had felt this way all along but tried her best to ignore it when Diane first starting asking her out. It was comforting to have a girlfriend again, a guaranteed date for Saturday night, to be part of a pair like so many other people. She could go out with her coupled friends and not feel like the fifth wheel, her friends no longer obliged to find her dates. She and Diane discussed marching together on Gay Pride Day, going to Provincetown on vacation or Cherry Grove for a long weekend. And as they'd rushed headlong into their attachment, making plans she suspected she would never keep, Jo had felt an emptiness building that made her wonder if there was anything inside her at all.

The night before, they'd been to a party where Jo had spent a lot of time talking to Annie, an acquaintance from the feminist newspaper she was active with. Jo had been immediately drawn to Annie's cool wit and intelligence but had never thought about her much because Annie had a lover. At the party she found that, all of a sudden, they were flirting with each other, talking earnestly about the next issue of the paper while smiling shyly and watching each other's mouths. Both of them blushed when Annie's girlfriend came back with a fresh drink. That night, exhilarated by the mutual attraction yet knowing probably nothing would come of it, Jo avoided going home with Diane or asking her back to her apartment. She claimed she felt sick, and Diane, who must have realized that meant no sex, gave in. "We'll just make up for it tomorrow night," Diane had whispered.

She didn't think Diane was in love with her. It was just a matter of convenience for both of them, Jo for companionship, however quiet, and Diane for sex and lots of it. Diane had recently ended a long-term relationship in which her lover had suggested they continue living together but be celibate.

"I tried it for two months," Diane had said, her twisted face reflecting the the pain that situation must have caused her. "Then I left. Sleeping in the other room after all those years—I just couldn't deal with it."

When Jo had said she'd once gone for two years without sex, Diane's face reflected a lack of understanding. She was silent for a few minutes, then finally said, "Wow," and then, after another long pause, "Where should we go for dinner?"

Now Diane was handing her two aspirin, not the whole bottle to fish them out herself, and a cold glass of water. She took them with a "Thanks," silently wishing she could have had three instead.

"What's up?" Diane asked, getting back into bed and fluffing up their pillows.

"What do you mean?" Jo asked, letting the sweating glass rest on her stomach.

"You seem pretty far away," Diane said, and Jo thought it was one of the most perceptive things she'd heard her say. Diane lay on her side facing Jo, her head in her hand. "So where are you?"

Jo took a sip of water and felt cool drops from the glass land on her chest. Diane smiled and rubbed them gently into her skin, her hand perilously close to Jo's breasts. She's going to try *again*, Jo thought.

"This isn't working," Jo said, before she realized what was coming out of her mouth.

"You should sit up to drink," Diane advised.

"No," Jo said firmly. "I mean *this*, this, you and me, this relationship."

Diane sat up, looking like someone had slapped her. "What's wrong with it?" and Jo knew by her tone that she honestly didn't know.

"We just don't connect in any way," Jo continued.

"We connected pretty well on the floor tonight," Diane said, smiling at the memory.

We connect so badly, Jo thought, she doesn't even know what I mean by not connecting. "I guess it's just not enough for me, the sex part. We don't talk," Jo elaborated.

"That's not true," Diane said, pouting and inching away slightly. "We *do* talk. We've only been going out a little while, and I know a lot about you, like about your job and your ex-lovers and your family and what kinds of stuff you like to do. How do I know those things, if we don't talk?"

"All right, so we do talk," Jo admitted, sorry for her choice of words. "But what does all this talk *tell* you about me?"

Diane looked more confused than ever and was probably

beginning to understand that whatever she said would be wrong.

"Don't worry," Jo was saying, "it's a rhetorical question." She slid over Diane onto the cat again, shimmied into her jeans and t-shirt.

"You can't leave at four in the morning. It's crazy. Just wait till it gets light," Diane said. But Jo ignored her, retrieving her shoes from under the bed and sitting down quietly to put them on. Diane added slyly, "Does this have anything to do with Annie Magill?"

Jo looked at her, shocked at the second perceptive question of the evening.

"I'm not stupid, you know," Diane said.

"No," Jo said, "no one said you are." She finished tying her laces and stood up, looking down at Diane. "Annie has a lover. You met her."

"Yeah, and you know my theory that everyone's in a constant state of breaking up," Diane said, with a cynical smirk.

"It's just me," Jo said, clumsily. "I'm just not good at this sort of thing. It isn't you or Annie or anyone but me. Really. I'm not good at casual sex."

"I'd say you were very good at it."

Jo, exasperated instead of flattered, snapped, "You know what I mean."

"You mean," Diane said, "that you're not in love with me."

Jo turned her glance out the window.

"But I'm not in love with you either," Diane said. "That's the beauty of it. We're just two dykes having a great time."

Jo smiled, wishing she could climb back into bed. What will I do, she wondered suddenly, next Saturday night? Couldn't they just continue this way for weeks, months even?

"You could just keep me around," Diane suggested, "till you find that girl of your dreams."

"I can't," Jo said finally. "It's making me too sad."

She put her hand on the doorknob, hesitated, and looked back over her shoulder. Diane was sitting with the sheet just under her breasts, staring at her sadly.

"If you change your mind, you know where I am," Diane said.

Jo nodded quickly as the doorknob turned in her hand.

Sex Among the Bukovacs

The first thing my father said to my mother as her husband was, "Now you're all mine." We have a picture of the moment right after he said it. They are standing in the cobblestone street in front of the church, her body pressed into his, their cheeks meeting in an ardent embrace, the sweeping train of her gown wrapped in front of them, holding them together. He whispers, just to her, then his best man snaps the picture, then they are untangled and surrounded by friends and family. They are swept away to a reception at his parents' house, with food and champagne bought by saving ration stamps for months. That night there is no honeymoon vacation, just a fulfillment of love in their furnished rooms, where my father will soon leave my mother to go off to war. But now she is his, now they kiss and caress and begin to create the life that will become my sister Kay's.

...

Sometimes I wonder if I have invented all of this. Because as far as I knew, my parents never had sex. Their bedroom door was always open, day or night, except for about twenty minutes on Sunday mornings, when they were getting dressed for church. That was invariably the time when I needed my mother desperately and would plaintively tap, tap, tap on the heavy door. "Just a minute," came my father's voice. "Mommy's getting dressed." I would go away, back to my room to try to deal with whatever was on my mind by myself. Then five minutes later I was knocking again, a persistent pestering designed to make my mother feel guilty for being twenty minutes behind a closed door. "Can I come in?" came my sad voice. "Not yet." When I was really little, I positioned myself outside the door, straining for sounds from inside, sitting in the hall staring up at the massive door and repeating "Mommy, can I come in yet?" over and over. My father finally opened the door and stepped over me. And so I learned that whining wears your mother down, that if you have the stamina for it, you will finally be let in behind that big door to watch in fascination as your mother hooks her stockings to her garter belt.

...

"69" was scratched into the top of my desk in fifth grade. I didn't do it. The desk behind mine said "Fuck" in the same unsteady hand.

That spring Sr. Marie Claire had separate conferences with the girls and the boys.

"Girls," she said when it was our turn, "some of you are becoming young women already, and I want to talk to you about wearing brassieres." Some of us, she advised, were developing breasts that bounced noticeably under our jumpers. She looked directly at me. I crossed my arms in my lap over my budding breasts. They suddenly felt enormous.

What did she talk to the boys about? I knew they had something down there, but I wasn't sure what. I knew I had something down there, too, but I wasn't sure what that was either. I did know it was sprouting a few hairs, and my father was no longer allowed to walk into the bathroom for his comb or electric razor when I was taking a bath.

Then there were the spots on my pajama bottoms.

Funny, brown spots forming no particular pattern. I tried to rub them out with the bar of Ivory in the bathroom, but they were still there. I stuffed the pajamas hopelessly into the laundry basket, thinking my mother might miss the stains if she threw everything quickly into the washer together.

But my mother was a careful washer. She checked for stains. She brought the pajamas in question into my bedroom on a Saturday morning when I was still rubbing the sleep from my eyes. She sat on the edge of my bed and looked puzzled.

"You tried to rinse out your pajamas," she said.

I burst into tears. "I'm sorry. I don't know how that stuff got on them."

She took a deep breath and let it out slowly. "Do you know what those stains are?"

I sniffled that I didn't.

She said, "They're blood," and got ready, I was sure, to tell me I was dying of an incurable disease, like Mimi Covino's little sister. "When a girl gets to be a certain age, once a month she bleeds down there. It's so you can have a baby. You tell me the next time it happens, and I'll show you how to use Kotex." She crumpled the pajamas and tucked them out of sight. "It just means you're growing up. My baby's growing up."

She left me with that thought, and the realization that Kotex, which I had already investigated in the bathroom closet, were not something you put over your breasts.

···

Before the brown stains got onto my pajamas, I wore them once to the drive-in movies with my parents. The movie was something adult, but they took me because they knew I wouldn't understand and would probably just fall asleep in the back seat. In the middle of the movie, I was still awake, and I saw one woman get into bed with another and begin kissing and stroking her. There was one bare breast on the screen, then another. I was fascinated.

"Put your head down, Robbie," my mother said, and my father turned off the sound.

...

On the school playground, our favorite game was War. The boys against the girls. The object was to take prisoners, and whoever took the most that day won. When the boys captured a prisoner, it was frightening. They dragged her up the playground hill and formed a tight circle around her. The boys' leader, Thomas Griffith, who was also the tallest and most handsome, pulled up her dress and spanked her bottom. The rest of the girls stared up the hill in horror and amazement as the circle formed and disbanded. My friend Alison Thorne was always getting dragged up the hill. She said it was not as bad as it looked. I was always clever and never got caught.

It was after Sr. Marie Claire found out about this game that she had her talks with us.

...

I thanked God that my grade school class would graduate in 1968, not 1969. Every time we heard a reference to 1969, or 69 books, or 169 people, the snickering started. I came to class one morning and found it scratched into my desktop. I tried to color it in with pencil, but the lead shimmered eerily against the wood and made it stand out even more. It was in an awkward place, in the top corner, not easily covered when I opened my books. Sometimes I put my hand over it, just so I wouldn't have to look at it.

"You don't know what '69' means?" Patty Bloomette scoffed. She knew everything about sex, because she had five older brothers.

"Tell me," I pleaded, tired of being embarrassed by a number I didn't understand.

She drew me toward her, her hot breath in my ear sending a quiver up my spine. "It's when... it's when a boy and a girl do bad things and then the girl has a baby!" She released me suddenly, giggled, and ran away.

That was the same definition she's given me for "fuck" and "blow job." It was all the same, and my parents had done it all. Three times.

...

Once when I was visiting my parents from my home in another state, my mother took me into her confidence.

"I'm worried about your father," she said softly, even though we were alone in the house. "I think he may be sick."

It was Saturday morning and she was still in bed. I had brought her a cup of coffee and was sitting on the edge of the bed.

"Why?" I asked.

"I don't know how to put this, and I wouldn't bring it up if I weren't worried, but, well, he's impotent," she said, "and that's a sign of diabetes. I read about it in my medical book. Diabetes is what your grandpap died of."

I was speechless. Not because of the possibility of illness. Because Dad couldn't get it up. And Mom wanted him to. They'd tried. It was a problem.

I cleared my throat and suggested she make a doctor's appointment for him and make him keep it. All the time thinking, they actually *do* have sex.

...

Miss Novak, our health and phys. ed. teacher, drew on the blackboard in different colors of chalk. She made the woman's vagina pink, the man's penis blue.

"I know a lot of you have gotten the wrong information about this," she said, peering across her bifocals directly at me. I crossed and uncrossed my legs and glanced over at Roseanne Graziano in the next row, who was the only girl I'd ever met with a freckle on her ear. I was fascinated by the way it moved when she yawned. She was my best friend in ninth grade. We learned the American Sign Language alphabet together from a picture chart in the dictionary, so that we could talk to each other in class without getting caught. Now Roseanne was signing "This is too weird" under her desk.

"There is only one way a girl can get pregnant, and you're looking at it," Miss Novak said in her no-nonsense way, inserting the blue penis into the pink vagina with a swirl of red chalk. "Not by French kissing, or from toilet seats, or by rubbing against each other. By sexual intercourse. Period." She underlined the drawing twice, then bored the information into us with her eyes. I thought I saw most of the heads in the room lower, or maybe it was just mine. Roseanne's ear turned pink, her freckle deepened to burgundy. She smiled at me shyly across the aisle, her hand poised in her lap for a message.

"How would she know?" she signed.

...

My relationship with David Armand in twelfth grade was a mistake. He had told Roseanne he wanted to meet Roberta Bukovac, so she arranged for us to meet at Luna's Pizza Parlor. But he had gotten me confused with someone else and was too shy and embarrassed to point out his blunder to Roseanne. He told me about it when we broke up, right before we both went off to college.

I still have a picture of David and me the summer after graduation. We are holding hands in front of Luna's, standing about two feet apart with our arms forming a deep "V."

We had a basic understanding. I understood that if he held my hand and kissed me on the cheek sometimes that he would pay for the movies and drive me around in his beat-up Volkswagen. He understood that it would never go further than that.

...

The first time I had sex was my freshman year in college, on the floor of my dorm room with a girl named Dale. We were on the floor, not because it was sexier or we couldn't make it to the bed, but because that was the year I had creaky springs. In the middle of it, someone tapped on my door, wanting to borrow my shampoo. We pretended we weren't there, and she finally went away.

Later that year I wrote my parents a letter. My mother was so excited to get it, she saved it to read to the whole family at Sunday dinner. That was how she, my father, my two sisters, their husbands, and my niece, who was still too young to understand, found out about me and Dale. Kay later said it was the longest meal she'd ever eaten. We have a picture of the moment just before they heard the news. They are all lifting their glasses of milk or water in a toast.

...

But I've invented that story for sure. I only wanted to have sex with Dale. The first time was really after college, with a woman named Maggie, and it was on the floor, because that's where her mattress was. No one interrupted us, and afterward we went out and ate potato pancakes at a restaurant and stole shy glances at each other over the apple sauce.

I came out to my family one by one, over the next five years. I did it in person, on the phone, in a letter. When I wrote to my parents, I never mentioned sex. I told them my lover Hope's name, but I called her my friend.

"They're queasy about sex," I explained to Hope. "They don't like it."

"Oh, I bet they like it very much, they're just afraid to," she said. I gave her a quizzical look. Had I told her about Nebraska, where my father was stationed for four months when he was first in the army? How my mother followed him there and sat in a rented room in a boarding house all day waiting for him to come to her in his off-duty hours? How she spoke of it as "obligation," but how her eyes shone as if she'd really meant to say "romance"? We have a picture of them outside the boarding house, their cheeks fused like in their wedding picture, as if they were one person in those days. "Nebraska," my mother printed in the border of the snapshot, but it could have been anywhere.

...

Not long after I sent them the letter, I got on a plane and surprised my parents. My father greeted me stiffly on the porch, and my mother ran into the bedroom and closed the door. My father went in after her.

I stood outside their door, my hand poised to knock on it. The last time I'd done this I had been eye-level with the doorknob. From inside I heard my mother blowing her nose, and the low, reassuring tone of my father's voice. As I brought my hand to my side, the doorknob turned, and my father stepped past me. My mother's pain was framed in the doorway. Her eyes were red and swollen. Her cheeks were dotted with pink blotches. Her bottom lip was trembling. She couldn't look up, for fear of what she'd see.

I spoke quietly, softly as a child.

She lifted her eyes and they darted over and around me before locking into mine. The terror drained from her face as if she'd peeled off a mask. If she had spoken, she probably would have said, Oh, Robbie, it's you. If I had thought about it, I might have taken a picture.

SHELTER

About ten o'clock the page in front of me started getting fuzzy, the words and letters blurring into each other to form one long nonsense word. I put down my red pencil. "I can't do this anymore. I bet I'm missing things," I said, taking off my glasses and rubbing my eyes till I was sure they were good and red.

Mariel looked up from the galleys she had hunched over for hours. "Just a little more, Cat. Maybe you and I should run out and get some coffee."

Beverly jumped up from her desk at the window. "There's some left in the can from last weekend. We could make it," she said.

Mariel and I exchanged raised eyebrows. At first, we had been the only two to show up for volunteer proofreading at the newspaper, and I had been secretly thinking I could make the most out of a bad situation. Mariel and I had been flirting with each other for a couple of weeks, ever since our eyes met at a weekly collective meeting in acknowledgment of some particularly racist remark by one of our sister feminists. I had never really noticed her before, but after that knowing, second-long glance, she was all I could think about. Unfortunately, both of us lacked the confidence to take that first hesitant step: "Would you like to have dinner this week?" "Want to see a movie?" "How about brunch sometime?" An evening of proofreading together, though it would be torturous for two women to check almost seventy galleys alone, might give our relationship the push it needed.

Then Beverly showed up. There is one like her in every feminist organization I've ever been in, with a personality that grates on everyone else like a dry pen over paper, who unfortunately is also extremely dependable. In one way, it was a relief, because she put a dent in the work, and as a professional proofreader, she was quick and accurate. On the other hand, there would be no being alone with Mariel, not even for a drink afterwards, unless we deceived Beverly, told her we weren't going anywhere but home and then made straight for a coffee shop or bar the minute she'd turned the corner. I was already planning to mention it to Mariel the next time Beverly went to the bathroom, hoping Mariel would think I was clever, not a cad. Possibly, I had misread Mariel and she would turn away in horror, saying, "But she's our *sister!*" and make me feel like I should go back to Feminism 101.

While Beverly was trying to figure out the coffee maker, an "antique" that we'd bought from a defunct leftie magazine, I was tapping my pencil to some song in my head, stealing sidelong glances at Mariel across the room. She was hunched over again, but she looked gorgeous, her face a study of intelligence and commitment. I was deep in a fantasy about kissing her in the moonlight, when another voice snapped me back to the office.

"Is somebody in charge here?" it asked again.

Beverly, standing beside the coffee she'd dumped on the floor, did not look in control. Mariel, with her finger marking her place on the galley, looked up unwillingly.

"We all are, sort of. We're a collective," I offered. "Well, we're a part of a collective."

"Hrmph," she said and stepped back out into the hall. All

three of us looked at each other. We'd had interesting or unusual people at the newspaper office before—disgruntled writers, performers demanding that their ads get prime placement on the calendar page, even Kate Millett, whom most of us hadn't recognized. This was our first street person.

She dragged in two shopping bags that looked like they were crammed with crushed newspaper and the plastic bags you get from the dry cleaner. She pulled the bags right into the middle of the room and propped them against each other. This took several tries, but finally the one that was mostly newspaper let the other sag against it. "So who do I talk to?" she asked, staring directly at me and ignoring the others.

"You can talk to me, that's fine," I said, hearing my voice get louder and drag out, like it did with small children and my eighty-five-year-old grandfather.

"You don't have to shout, I'm not deaf," she snapped, fumbling in her dress pocket for something. I studied her face as she did—it didn't match the raspy voice, the missing tooth, the grey-streaked hair. She was probably no more than forty.

"Where is it?" she mumbled, going back and forth between her safety-pinned pockets, pulling out a wadded Kleenex, scraps of aluminum foil, and a few pennies, all of which she examined and replaced. "They stole it," she said, looking first at me with terror and then at Beverly behind her, frozen at the coffee maker. "Can I have some coffee?" she asked, suddenly changing subjects.

"Certainly," I said. "Is it ready, Bev?"

Beverly looked confused by the simple question. "No, but it will be. If you wait a few minutes." She inched over to her desk.

"Would you like to sit down and wait for it?" I asked,

pointing to a chair. She eyed me suspiciously, then began rummaging through one of her bags, making them both fall over.

She pulled out a few battered pieces of paper torn from a stenographer's pad and said with relief, "Here it is. I thought they mighta got this, too." She stood the bags upright again. "Can I see that pencil?"

"Sure," I said, more accommodating than I was used to being. I leaned forward and handed it to her, but instead of using it, she tossed it into one of her bags.

"I want to put a letter in your paper," she said. "Here it is." She walked toward me, shooting a glance back at her bags and at Mariel, who, not having said a word, must have seemed particularly suspicious. She stopped halfway to my desk and said, "Wait, I gotta bring my bags."

"It's okay to leave them there," I said, trying to sound reassuring. "No one will touch them, really."

"Ha," she snorted. " I heard *that* before," and she pulled them toward my desk and leaned them against it. "Here's the letter I want you to print."

I slowly uncrinkled and flattened the sheets onto my desk. "I'm Cat," I said. "And that's Mariel and Beverly. We work as a group, can they read it, too?"

"Hrmph," she said, frowning in their direction. "Oh, why not?"

"What's your name?" Mariel asked, standing behind me to read over my shoulder.

"It's right there, in plain English," she snapped, and my eyes traveled down to the signature.

"Helen Leveritt," I read aloud for the others. "Well, we'll just take a few minutes now to read this, Helen."

"Hrmph," Helen said again. "Is that coffee ready yet?" It was, and Beverly got her a styrofoam cup of it. "What, no milk?" Helen demanded, and Beverly took it back and put some Cremora in it. "You should use real milk, who knows what crap they put in that stuff. The government invented stuff like that to spread cancer to poor people."

"We don't have a refrigerator," Beverly explained.

"Then get one," she said, disgusted. "You got money, don't you?" She pointed to my desk. "You got an IBM typewriter, don't you? Well, don't you? I guess that means you can have real milk." She fished through her bags and pulled out half a sandwich, the ready-made kind from bus stations and automats. Pulling the plastic wrap off it, she dunked it into her coffee,

I was so distracted I had only gotten through the first line of the letter, "To Mayor Koch," but Mariel had read the whole thing and taken a chair next to me. I read on.

This is to inform you of the deplorable conditions at the East 6th Street shelter for women.

It went on for two clearly written and understandable pages, double-sided, describing how she, as a resident of the shelter, had tried on two different occasions to organize the residents to demand better treatment. The shelter, she said, was filthy. One night she had found a rat in the bathroom. The food was inedible, and most of the residents were losing more weight than they had on the streets. When she tried to get people to speak up, the administration first hid her belongings, then slipped something into her food that made her violently ill for two days. Finally, she was thrown out and told they couldn't find her possessions. She was imploring Mayor Koch to do something about what was going on, not just there, but in shelters all over the city.

I finished and handed the letter to Beverly.

"You believe me, don't you?" Helen asked, without any of her former aggression. "I'm not crazy, y'know."

"I know that, Helen," I said. "We all know that." But why was I still talking slowly and deliberately, as if she couldn't understand me?

"Look," she said, a look of sudden panic on her face, "I brought my credentials." Out of her bag she pulled a yellowed copy of the newsletter of the local branch of the Socialist Workers Party. "They didn't get this. I kept this under my pillow." She waved it in front of us impatiently. "Here, look at it, for Chrissake."

It was dated 1971, and the front page article was titled, "What Women Have Contributed to the Socialist Party." The byline was Helen Leveritt. I skimmed it quickly, taking just enough time to notice the lucidity of the prose, which matched, if not surpassed, that of the letter.

"Not bad writing, huh?" she said, proudly, and leaned over to point to her byline. As she did so, she shoved her coffee, with bits of sandwich floating in it, right under my nose. "If I was good enough to write for them, I guess I can get a letter printed *here*."

I started to speak but found I was letting Mariel talk over me. "It's not the kind of thing we normally print," she was explaining, in an even tone she reserved for rejected writers, those who were not quite up to snuff. "We could get in a lot of trouble with a letter like that."

"But it's true!" Helen said, the angry tone returning.

"We'd love to have a well-researched piece on the shelters," Mariel continued, and I shuddered. I had no idea what I would have said if I'd spoken first, but I only hoped it would have been different. "In fact, one of our reporters is interested in doing that kind of piece and might want to talk to you about your experiences. Maybe you could call her from here."

"What the fuck!" Helen exploded, ripping the letter out of Beverly's hands. "Who the fuck do you think you are? You think I'm crazy, don't you?"

"No, Helen, not at all," I offered, still in my talking-to-a-crazy-person voice.

"Hrmph," she said, pulling the newsletter away from me and stuffing both the letter and the article back into her bags. "Feminists," and she spat the word out onto the floor near my feet. "If I were dressed different, you'd print this letter. If I wasn't on the streets, you'd listen to me then. You think I'm crazy, don't you? Don't you?" Her voice was approaching a scream.

"It wouldn't matter," Mariel said, "how you were dressed. We just can't print inflammatory stuff like this. Not if it isn't researched."

"Researched!" she laughed, and the sound vibrated off the walls. "Sister, you wouldn't know research if it came and sat on your face! I don't need no dykes telling me they can't print my letters!" She spat again, this time in Mariel's direction. We all stayed in our places, riveted to the spot by fear of her sudden violence.

Helen dropped her empty coffee cup into one of her bags and picked both of them up. She took one last look at us as she headed for the door, mumbling all the way. "You call this a newspaper?" "Not a writer in the bunch." "Fucking queers." Mariel opened her mouth to say something, then closed it. At the door Helen turned around and asked aggressively, "Anybody got a dollar for carfare?"

The others shrugged, while I jumped up, fished one remaining bill out of my wallet, and handed it to her. She looked at it with disgust. "Whatsa matter with you? You don't know the difference between a buck and a twenty?" She shook her head, while I stood stupidly with the twenty dollar bill stretched out toward her. "Keep it, you'll need it, believe me," she said. "You think you're safe, here in this nice office, but they can get you. They got me." At the last minute, she snatched the twenty from my hand and laughed in her chilling way. Her mumbles of "dykes" and "feminist schmeminist" echoed down the hall.

When I turned around, Beverly and Mariel were helping themselves to coffee.

"Jeez," Beverly said, "I thought the door downstairs was locked after nine."

"We should talk to the building manager about that," Mariel agreed. "Really, they up our rent thirty percent and then we're verbally abused in our own space! If she hadn't been a homeless woman, I would've let her have it."

I took coffee, black, sadly and guiltily going back to my desk. I got out another red pencil to replace the one I'd given Helen. I glanced at Mariel with new indifference. The intrigue was gone, as quickly as it had started between us. My thoughts were no longer on deceiving Beverly to get Mariel alone, and when Beverly went to the bathroom minutes later, I said nothing. I didn't know what to say. We couldn't have gone anywhere, even if I'd still wanted to. I'd just given away my last twenty.

Voyages Out 1

Carla Tomaso

Kat

I read in a magazine recently that with practice you can control what goes on in your dreams. All you have to do is realize while you're dreaming that you are having a dream and then you can tell it what you want it to do. I don't approve. I think that takes all the fun out of it—like knowing what sex the fetus is or hearing how the movie turns out while you're on the way to see it. So you watch the movie and calculate how all the effects add up. A satisfying intellectual exercise, maybe, but it's not really living. I had a dream about my stepsister, Kat, where she was swimming in a pond and then started to drown right before my eyes. I stood on the shore and watched. As she went down for the last time, I asked myself—is this a dream? The thing is that it didn't matter. One pale arm shot into the air from the glassy surface of the water and I stood fixed, rooted on the shore like a tree, dream or no dream.

The first story I ever wrote was about my relationship with Kat. The central symbol shivered with adolescent angst, a glass bird. There was a struggle and eventually the bird was broken. The symbol was, I suppose, about the terrible fragility of our relationship. The story won my high school literary prize and I became a sort of troubled, sensitive celebrity, my purpose in writing the thing, no doubt.

Several people gave me glass birds that Christmas which I stood in a row on my bedroom dresser.

Now, twenty years later, things haven't really changed much. If anything, they've gotten worse. Kat and I almost never speak and when we do, usually on my side with a frenzied resolve to be friends, for God's sake, to act like adults, Kat hurts my feelings and makes me so angry I never want to see her again. I don't have any idea how she feels about me but I imagine the experience isn't very pleasant for her either.

"What does it feel like?" I ask Kat one morning when I'm fourteen and she's seventeen. She's been out all night with her boyfriend, David, not for the first time or even the twenty-first time, but now I really want to know. Why now? Because at a mixer a boy has asked me to dance and then has asked to kiss me at the door to the bus hired to take the girls back home. I didn't want to particularly, but I had a sense of inevitability about that and everything else I supposed came after it. I wasn't yet aware that I had any choice in the matter of love-making and it certainly hadn't occurred to me that the gender of the person with whom I did "it" could be a consideration.

Kat is brushing her long and wavy blonde hair in front of the mirror and I am sitting on the edge of her bed. We share a room. I'm supposed to cover for her when she stays out all night. She's very responsible. She gives me the number where she'll be and finds out if I'll be home all night (where else would I be?) so if anything goes wrong she can call me to help her. She never has yet and her mother and my father, who have been married for two years, haven't caught her climbing in the window at six in the morning. I think

they'd rather not know what goes on with Kat for fear
they'd have to do something about it.

"It's kind of strange, at first, especially if the boy doesn't
know what he's doing."

"Does David?" I ask, trying unsuccessfully to imagine
anyone ever doing it, let alone well.

"Of course David knows what he's doing. He's been
doing it forever." David is eighteen and has a sweet bony
face and a pleasant manner. Best of all, he's real nice to me
whenever I go anyplace with him and Kat in his beige convertible. Still, David seems like a tall little boy and the
thought of him having done "it" forever makes me smile.

"It feels good," Kat continues, her face milky with recent
memory. "Like," she shakes out of it, "you're being filled
up with somebody else. And then sometimes you have an
orgasm."

"Oh God," I say. "What's that?"

"It's like the entire area down there is sneezing. It's fun.
You want to go out on a date with us next weekend? Alan
thinks you're cute. I'll ask him to take you." Alan is a
boyfriend of Kat's who hangs around still, just because he
likes "her act," as he puts it. Kat is wonderful; I think so,
too. She is great-looking and says whatever she wants like
she owns the whole world. I get good grades, have intense
relationships with girlfriends, in reality, and with teachers,
in fantasy, and do not particularly enjoy it next Saturday
night when Alan gently kisses me in the backseat of David's
car. We're all a little drunk, me for the first time, and the
date seems like a dream of being slightly seasick on a foggy
ocean liner. But I know that Kat will protect me. And she
does. She tells David to drive us home and then she puts me
to bed before sneaking out the window to spend the night
with him. I love her.

Five years later, Kat is married to somebody else, somebody she fights with but seems to like and I am visiting her from college. We are still on speaking terms although we've had some major disagreements in the interim. What about? Kat getting drunk, doing drugs, yelling at our parents. Except, as I recall, I never bring up these things with her; she just automatically assumes I'm on the side of the parents, partly because I still live with them when I'm home and partly because nothing in my life is like hers. I still think she's wonderful, but now something in her scares me. She's angry in a way I don't think I'll ever understand.

We are talking about sex again. I still haven't had it. Kat is pregnant. I am thinking that I want to have sex, but I have to talk around and around the issue. "I have a friend at college," I say earnestly, "who does foreplay with her dates so she can have orgasms. After she has one she tells the guy to take her home. I warn her she's going to get raped if she doesn't watch out."

"Why doesn't she just have intercourse?" Kat asks. I'm beginning to realize that she thinks this "friend" is me. She isn't. The truth is that she's the woman I'm in love with.

"Doesn't want to get pregnant or any diseases, I guess," I say. "Her home is on a farm in Connecticut," I add irrelevantly, "and she lives in my dorm."

Then Kat surprises me. "Well, good for her. No reason to do it if all you want is an orgasm. She ought to do the boy, though. You're right."

"Because he might get angry and hurt her," I say, trying to sound dispassionate. "It's only fair."

"Exactly," Kat says, but already she is thinking about something else. She has put her open hands on top of her belly right under her breasts, as if she is warming the baby. Soon after she delivers, a few weeks later, her stomach is completely flat, as if nothing was ever in there at all.

"It will happen soon," she says finally. "I bet there are

lots of boys at that college of yours who would love to spend some time in bed with you."

The idea seems so preposterous I nearly laugh out loud, but I'm not ready to explain anything to Kat yet—my inexpressible boredom with the concerns of the boys I've dated, the all-night talks I stage with the woman I love but haven't yet told, the fantasies I've had since before I knew Kat at all. Would she understand? I convince myself that she would and even stage scenarios in my mind where she embraces me and tells me it's wonderful, that she wishes she had the courage to love women like I do.

While I'm away at graduate school Kat has a second child and a few months later flips out. Her husband puts her in the university psychiatric hospital where his brother is a psychiatrist. When she goes home, after about three weeks, she calls me at my dorm, something she has never done before. She sounds different, more peaceful, and I wonder if they have put her on tranquilizers. Finally she tells me that she's seeing a psychiatrist named Beth whom she really likes. "The next time you come home," she says, "I'll see if you can meet her. It's more like we're friends than client and therapist. Last week she walked behind my chair and put her hands on my shoulders." On the strength of this, I begin to write Kat about Ann, my lover. I call her "my wonderful new friend" and let it go at that. The next time I come home Kat tells me she's terminated her therapy. We never talk about it again.

As years pass things begin to matter less. There are fewer and fewer first times for anything—first date, first sex, first job, first house, first affair—and none of these except for that first date do I really share with Kat. I try a couple of times but she seems to be afraid of me, as if what I tell her will reach out and grab her by the throat. She comes to visit me and Ann at our cottage in the mountains. She has divorced her first husband and is in love with a forty-five-year-old man who wears a ponytail and an earring shaped like a ship's anchor. The three of us talk and drink for hours. I tell Kat the man she's describing reminds me of David; I tell her I'm glad she's divorced; I tell her what she wants to hear. She and Ann smoke a joint and analyze Kat's mother, my stepmother, while I wash dishes. I hear them say things like: "she's got a control issue," "she doesn't respect women," "pulls you in and then drops you down." Ann is a psychotherapist and Kat is into alternative types of healing as well as sex therapy, so they have a lot in common. Kat hasn't done any sex therapy yet, but she's taking classes at the community college where they show films of all gender combinations making love in every way imaginable. Sometimes the students laugh, Kat says, but you aren't really supposed to.

I get the feeling that no one in my family approves of my living arrangements but that no one is willing to disapprove either. Kat says she knew all along that I was going to be a lesbian. When she says it, blowing the steam from her coffee cup away from her face, I catch a note of superiority which annoys me and I can't think of a way to get her back.

"How could you have?" I say. "I didn't even know myself." It's not exactly the tack I want but it will do.

"You never really liked dating," she says smugly. "And then all these letters from college about Ann. It was obvious." Our black and white cat jumps onto her lap, turns around twice and then jumps off. Kat takes a sip of coffee. Ann looks uncomfortable, waiting for me to say something.

"I disappointed you." To say this I have had to muster up every reservoir of self-confidence I have.

She sighs and I know I've lost her. "To each her own," she says, giving me a mock salute. "I think you guys are great."

Kat sleeps on the couch in the living room and in the morning she is gone before either Ann or I awaken. On the bed she leaves her blanket neatly folded and a note about the neighbor's coming by to check on a dead cat they've found. It wasn't ours. Kat writes at the bottom that she's got a long drive ahead of her and "thanks for a great evening." I notice that she's used the word "great" twice this visit to describe things she didn't like at all.

A few weeks later I'm sitting in the kitchen at my father and stepmother's house when Kat decides to tell me the truth. She admits that she couldn't sleep. She says she heard squeaking noises from Ann's bedroom and thought Ann was coming on to her all the way from in there.

"Are you kidding?" I say. My stepmother is stirring split pea soup at the stove and can't hear us. From the back I notice that her shoulders are wide, just like Kat's, and I suddenly feel out-of-place. I don't belong in this house full of gigantic blonde women who have babies and take care of men.

"For God's sake," I whisper. "That's nuts."

"I know," she says half-heartedly. I can tell she still believes it happened. That night I ask Ann about it and for a crazy moment hope that maybe Kat had it figured right.

After that, Kat ceases to exist for me in the present. I comfort myself with memories. My father and stepmother report on her as if she were a movie star or a foreigner. "Kat is going to nursing school; Kat and Bill split up; Kat and Bill are back together." I see her once a year at most.

Bill turns out to be very scary, the kind of person who puts an arm around you while he whispers something vaguely hostile in your ear. The kind of man who wears long hair and an earring and hates homosexuals. But he doesn't say that; he says he knows lots of them and while he can't understand what they do, he certainly applauds their right to do whatever they want. Kat lights a cigarette and puts it in his mouth. We are sitting around a large wooden table at the beach house they are subletting from a friend. Bill rubs Kat's upper thigh and tells us how they like to experiment with their sexuality. Kat smiles and explains how inhibited she was before she met Bill.

"What do you two do in bed?" Bill asks Ann after about six beers. "If you don't mind me asking." I stand up to go and they follow us to the door. Bill has his arm around Kat and she sways a little, laughing. I look into her eyes, thinking: This is absolutely your last chance, but I see nothing there except my own reflection.

Kat taught me many things, most of which I have never used. She taught me to drive and to accelerate around the curve, something I do use. She taught me how to put on makeup. I would watch her in front of her mirror applying base coat, eyeliner, blusher and mascara as if her life depended on it, as if she had a hideous facial deformity instead of perfect features. She taught me to listen to the Romantics, Aaron Copland, Barbra Streisand. She taught me to smoke Tareytons and fast the first day of a diet so my stomach would shrink. She was the first really troubled person I ever knew. She'd gotten into a knife fight once when

she was in boarding school and had a scar under her right elbow to prove it. She hated some people and loved others
with a thunderous passion that used up most of her life. I
thought she knew more about the real stuff than anybody
I'd ever met.

Kat and Bill are back together now and Ann and I are visiting Kat in their new house. Her two kids live with them
but right now nobody but Kat is home. She is wearing tight
jeans and her thick hair still falls down her back in waves.
There isn't any gray in it. She smokes a cigarette and shows
us all the rooms they are remodeling. Bill has torn out the
ceiling to reveal the structural elements—her daughter's
room is decorated in a ballet motif with ballerinas on the
wallpaper and toe shoes blown up in a huge poster on the
wall. I remember that Kat used to dance. I admire her large
strong hands and her high cheekbones while she tells me
about Erin's successes in dancing school. I am reliving the
feelings I had for her when we were younger, a dangerous
activity, but for some reason I am hopelessly mired in
nostalgia.

"You could have been a dancer, Kat," I say. I want to tell
her that I once thought she was the best person on earth.
Right now, in Erin's bedroom, I wish she would do something so grand I could forget about the hard years in between.

"This dancing stuff is a pain," Kat says. "I have to drive
her all over town for performances and stuff and she's getting to be a little snot. Full of herself, like you were," she
says to me, "with all your straight A's and preppie girlfriends."

"Erin's ballet teacher is a lesbian," I say suddenly. "Ann's
cousin knows her." We walk back down the hall and I stare
up at the beams and ducts Bill has exposed.

"Jesus Christ," Kat says. "They're all over. I hope she doesn't try anything with Erin."

Ann has to drive home because I'm crying and screaming at the same time. We never say good-bye. Ann and I just continue to walk down the hall and out into the street.

"I didn't mean anything about you," Kat calls after us. "I love you no matter what you do."

I had another dream about Kat, right after the incident at her house. There was nothing complicated about it at all. We were making love. Right in the middle I realized that I was dreaming and I felt this incredible pressure to make myself stop. But I didn't. I was enjoying it too much.

It isn't until several weeks later on the telephone that I'm able to say to Kat what I need to say.

"I'm not doing anything wrong," I say finally. "So there's nothing for you to accept." As simple as that. There is silence on the other end. I can hear her breathing. I wish I could find the thing that will lead us softly back to the time when we trusted each other. But maybe, I am thinking as Kat says, "Of course not," it only worked because back then Kat was the one who knew everything.

I Love You More Than Anything

People are always asking me real suddenly like they've been preoccupied for half an hour working up the nerve—"So, hey, Ginny, what do you do all day?" They're surprised, I guess, that a thirty-one-year-old college graduate with no kids or visible artistic drive stays home on purpose. What they don't know is that my parents left me a little money and weeding the tomatoes or brewing a cup of tea can take me an entire happy hour.

And it never fails that Jule, if she's there, answers for me, "She does a lot of stuff. She's a very creative person. She works harder than I do." Jule's trying to help but the way she says it, especially this last time when Vicki and Kate were visiting, makes it sound like there really is something wrong with me. After our friends leave I go up to my room and slam the door to think about it. I lie on my bed and stare at the horizontal strips of pale light on the wall coming through the open levolors. But it's not like I'm in prison. In fact my room is perfect, just the way I want it, and Jule likes it too when she comes to visit.

I watch the levolor shadows and feel completely alone even though the cat has wrapped herself around my feet. All of a sudden I realize that this is the same feeling I had when I was a kid and my parents would leave me to go off to a family party because I'd said I didn't want to go when I really did.

"She doesn't want to come, she doesn't have to come." I can still hear my father shouting this loudly from the bottom of the stairs to make sure I get the point. "Let her stay home all day with nothing to do. What do we care?" He knew to say that because he used to do the same thing when he was a kid. "Let her eat eggs with grandpa," were his final words on the subject. As soon as I heard the gravelly sound of their tires I'd go to the window with an empty heart and watch the whole day go by without me. There was no grandpa and no eggs. When my father stayed home as a kid the only other person left behind would be his grandpa, an old man with no teeth. That explains the part about the eggs.

The phone rings. Jule and I have separate phone numbers so I kind of hope it's her, calling to make up. I hope it's her and I hope it isn't. If it is her it means I can't lie on my bed and look at the lines of light on my wall and feel sorry for myself anymore. I'll have to say, "Yes, I understand," "No, I'm not mad anymore," "I'll try to express my feelings directly instead of slamming the door," etc. etc. I roll over on my stomach and answer on the third ring. I say, "Hi." The voice on the other end says, "Elizabeth?" I say "Who?" and he says "Elizabeth, isn't this Elizabeth?" "No," I say. "You've got the wrong number." "This sure sounds like Elizabeth," he says and I say, "Sorry."

After I hang up I go downstairs and hug Jule like we're old friends and nothing's happened. I make a silent resolution that I won't run away from things anymore like a child. I'm going to meet life head on. Jule smiles at me and I cry a little and we have dinner. It's catfish with green beans and red potatoes.

The first thing I do is to go out and get a job. It's at a counseling center for troubled adolescents which means that they've broken some law and their parents don't have much money. The reason I got the job is that my college degree is in educational counseling and also that nobody else applied.

My second day on the job (the first day they gave me a desk and told me what to do) a heavyset sixteen-year-old named Jeani tells me, while we're waiting in line at Burger King, that she wishes she had hair like mine. My hair is reddish brown and I usually wear it in a thick braid down my back. Then she stands on my foot. "Shit," I say, "ouch" and I pull my foot out from under hers, which works except that my Birkenstock doesn't come with it. "What the hell did you do that for?" I scream at her. A group of eight kids and two of us counselors are on our way back from a trip to the zoo and several of the kids are wearing t-shirts with the face of a gorilla or a rhino on the front. Everybody stops talking and looks at me. Jeff, the other counselor, walks over and kind of shakes his head. "Let's everybody be friends," he says and then goes back to the front of the line and orders a Whopper and a large fries. I have to bend over to take my sandal from under Jeani's foot. The way I do it is I lift her shoe up by the heel with one hand and slide mine out with the other. She must have balanced all her weight on the other foot for a moment because somehow she didn't fall on top of me.

Because of my resolution, I don't quit and besides, the job gets better after that. Two days before the appointment I have set up with her, we get word that Jeani and her family have moved up to New Hampshire. And then I get so busy doing counseling, taking the kids on outings to the beach and the mountains and finishing paperwork, that sometimes I'm gone from home twelve hours a day. Surprisingly I enjoy being busy. Jule complains but I tell her didn't she want me to work? Now we have something to say to people who ask me what I do all day.

Jule has a job with the phone company where she does all the same things the men do. She climbs poles and rewires telephone lines and installs telephones in people's houses.

That's one reason we each have our own line and three instruments apiece. Jule says she's lucky that the men on the job (and she's the only woman in our area) all like her because of the fact that she's such a good worker. It could have gone either way because so many men see a competent woman as a big threat.

But, because she's so good, Jule often gets home early, sometimes by two or three on a slow day, and if I'm not home until seven or eight, she really feels it. She goes through my closet to find shirts that need ironing or she washes the refrigerator door and the hood over the stove. She may install a new water-saving mechanism in the toilet bowl. She writes long journal entries about the disappointments of life and the insignificance of people. When I get home she sometimes reads me what what she's written and I feel bad, like if I was home earlier or if I could be nicer she would be writing about the significance of people and the rewards of life.

We eat dinner in front of television and Jule talks about whatever show we're watching and then she lies down with her head on my lap and falls asleep. While she sleeps I watch the next show, muting the sound by remote control so she won't wake up. I study her soft mouth and her chin and her wide forehead. Her face is so familiar to me it could be mine. An hour or so later I say, "Come on honey, time for bed" and her eyelids flicker and then open, but her eyes don't focus because she's still a little bit in that other world and she doesn't want to leave it yet.

That's the way it is every night unless we go out or somebody comes over. If somebody comes over we have dinner and then play a board game. We usually get real competitive and worked up, especially if we play teams. One night Vicki and Kate come over. We haven't seen them since the time Kate asked me what I did all day. They don't want to play a game at all; they just want to talk because everybody is real tired. They own a women's bookstore and the stress of making it work keeps them awake at night. Jule tells about our separate bedrooms as if they're the answer to sleep problems, as if she is real proud of the arrangement when I know for a fact that she's never even remotely liked the idea except when she's got the flu and her skin hurts.

Kate says, "Mind your own business." Jule shuts up and I just look at them.

Vicki is about forty-five and has a Rubenesque body and wavy brown hair. She wears beautiful fabrics that flow around her body suggestively, like they're gauzy curtains promising more. Kate is straightforward and ten years younger. She jogs and lifts weights and is proud of the way her arm muscles ripple when she picks up heavy books in the store. Jule and I are more alike. In fact sometimes people can't tell us apart when we answer the phone. They'll say, "Hi, which one is this?" and whichever one it is will tell them and then the conversation will start.

Vicki and Kate are real glad I'm working because it gives us all something new to talk about. We've sort of worn out the phone company and although there is lots to talk about with the bookstore Vicki and Kate seem to think that most of it is confidential. Maybe they're right because the clientele in a woman's bookstore is different from other bookstores. And if somebody wants a book on alcoholism or lesbianism or incest or they want to talk about it, they'd probably be glad the owner isn't running off and blabbing about it at dinner parties. But, it means I have to do all the talking about the counseling center and the staff and the kids. Maybe the stories about the kids should be confidential too, but nobody says anything and I don't care. I change the kids' names, though, just in case.

I tell a story about one girl who had been raped by a bunch of older boys and one about a boy whose mother put cigarettes out on his arms and about a gang of kids who stole cars and sold the parts for spending money. I try to make the stories entertaining and novel but they end up being just plain sad. And it's funny because when I work there and listen to the kids or take them out or do paperwork, it's not sad at all. I guess it's just telling the stories out of context and focusing on them that makes it all sound so bad.

"How in God's name can you work in a place like that?" Kate says. She's all curled up next to Vicki like a slender Siamese, watching everything through half-closed eyes.

"I have to go to the bathroom," Vicki says, untangling herself from her clothes and from Kate. Kate sits up and points her toes at me. Her calves ripple a few times before she puts her legs down on the coffee table.

"It's nice there," I say. "I feel like I'm helping the kids. We've been to the zoo three times." Kate's really beginning to piss me off. It's like she's got this thing about my having to justify myself all the time. "Just leave me alone about it," I say real loud, sounding like somebody else.

"She gets home late every night," Jule says, getting on the bandwagon. It's like she hasn't heard how mad I am at all. She's sitting by the fireplace and every so often she carefully pushes a log around or adds a piece of kindling. When she tells about my being late she throws a big log right in the center of the fire so that the pyramid of wood underneath it completely flattens out.

"You're gonna have to rebuild that," I say.

"Shut up," she says, "I know."

When Vicki comes back Kate says, "We have to go." I look at Jule but she's already busy working on the fire.

Then Jule and I sit in front of the fire and drink wine and I try to dig deep and say everything I'm feeling, as clearly as possible. I figure that I'll set the example and when she sees how well it works she'll want to do it too.

When I say, "I love you more than anything," she stares into the fire and grunts.

I say, "... but you're angry at me for things I can't help, like getting home late at night."

She says, "And not sleeping in the same bed as me."

"I can't help that either," I say, "honest to God. It's just this thing I have about my own space. You always visit me as much as you want."

"Well go to therapy then," she says straight into the fire-place.

"I do," I say, which obviously she knows. The big thing I've gotten out of it so far is that my neuroses don't make me sick and unnatural; they make me interesting.

"There are certain things I don't like," she says. She blows on some kindling so the rebuilt fire will catch.

I wait to see if there's anything else. There isn't, so I say, "You do love me?"

She says, "Yes," but she waits a long time to say it as if, even though it's the truth, that's the last thing she wants to tell me right now.

The next day as usual I go through a lot of small towns driving to work. I could take the highway and save a few minutes but I like the way the back roads make me feel. The towns have names ending in "borough" and "ham" and usually I can see a white steeple peeking out from pine trees on a hill or in the center of town behind a long grassy lawn if the road goes that way. I also see lots of statues of dead patriots. I think about how one of us, Jule or I, will hold the other's hand when she's dying and say, "Don't worry, I'm right beside you."

The first thing I do when I get to work is to look at the chart on the wall where they write our appointments and assignments. I'm supposed to see Andy, who's gotten in trouble again, this time for stealing a car and wrecking it on the same day. I'm supposed to help him see how to do things differently which, given his life, is going to take all the imagination I have. Mark, my boss, comes up behind me and says, "How was the commute?"

"Fine," I say.

"You oughta stick to the highway," he says and then, "Come to my office, would you?"

I figure he isn't going to fire me if he is telling me about changing my commuting route but I'm nervous anyway. He leans against the front of his desk as if this won't take long so I just stand there and wait to hear what he has to say.

"Ginny," he says, "Jeff's going back to school so I'd like you to take his place. You'll get a couple thousand more than you do now. Ok?" I tell him ok, without even thinking about it and then he sticks his hand out for me to shake. I grip it real tight because I like Mark even if he dresses in polyester pants that he hitches up with a tight belt above his waist. He's always bringing us books and articles and things that he's come across about our special interests. He thinks my special interest is small towns because of the route I take to get to work. "He'll train you starting the fifteenth," he says and I move to leave. "You're doing a great job," he pats me on the back. "I almost forgot to tell you."

Then I see Andy and we try talking about his dreams for the future: astronaut, film star, senator. He gets real excited about each job but not because of anything intrinsic to the work. "How much does a senator make?" he asks me. "How much for an astronaut?"

"You have to go to school and study all the time," I tell him. "You have to be totally honest."

"I'll be a movie star," he says. "I think that's more in line with my overall character. My girlfriend says my profile makes her wet. What do you think?" He turns his head sideways and I punch him in the arm.

Andy promises he'll try out for the George Chakaris part in West Side Story, which his high school is putting on as their fall play. I figure it's the next logical step on the hope-

ful new path we've sketched out for his future. For the first
time since I've been at this job, I get depressed. What good
are any of us doing, anyway, getting these kids all interested
in hope? Andy won't get the part, and if he does he'll never
be on time for rehearsals. He'll be in the federal penitentiary
by the time he's twenty-one and there's nothing I can do
about it. I tell everybody I have a headache and that I'm going home. I put papers in my bag and get in my car.

I decide to take the highway because I want to get home
as fast as I can. I feel better already. I want to surprise Jule
by showing her that, even though she wasn't direct, I really
heard her last night. After driving a half an hour, I go into
the liquor store near our house to buy sandwiches for lunch
and a bottle of $15.95 champagne. There's a line of con-
struction workers in front of the sandwich counter and I
keep shifting my weight and wondering when Jule will
come home from work today and if she'll be excited to see
me.

All the guys order variations of turkey sandwiches,
turkey and swiss, turkey and tomatoes. When it finally gets
to be my turn I ask for one tuna and one roast beef to give
the kid behind the counter some variety. He shows me the
beef. "This ok?" he asks. It's nice and red so I tell him it's ok
and to slice it thin.

When he's done the kid says, "Here you go," and hands
me two bags over the top of the counter. He looks about the
same age as Andy, except that he must be older if he's not in
school at noontime. I wonder if he dropped out and this is
the only job he could get.

"Thanks," I say. "They look really good." He smiles a
big toothy smile and I change my mind and decide that he's
in acting school at night or in an equity waiver production
of *Jesus Christ Superstar*. Maybe there's hope after all for
everybody including Andy and me.

I've been with Jule eleven years and all of a sudden it

seems like today could be the first day. Everything feels so special: the careful way the sandwich guy sliced the beef, piling a little red mound on wax paper after he ran it through the slicer; my promotion; the midday sunlight shining on the whiskey bottles in the front window as I walk out.

Jule's phone truck is parked on the street so I sneak up the stairs with the sandwiches and champagne to surprise her. I figure that work must have been slow so she's come home to take a nap. By the time I reach the top of the stairs I realize that somebody is in the bedroom with her, somebody I know. I don't go any further because I don't want to see things I'll have to remember the rest of my life.

"I'm home early Jule and Kate," I shout as loud as I can, "and now I'm going to sit on the back porch and eat my sandwiches." I turn and go back down the stairs and out to sit on the porch.

I spend a long time deciding which sandwich is going to be mine. While I decide, I open the champagne and drink long swallows from the bottle. The cat comes out to see what I'm doing and when it's clear that I'm not going to feed her, she begins to clean her tail. All at once I realize that I'm hungrier than I've ever been, that my stomach feels like an enormous hole maybe not even two sandwiches can fill. I take a bite of the roast beef.

Twenty years from now Jule and I will talk about this time and laugh about me eating the sandwiches while she is dressing and rushing Kate out the front door. "Like bad slapstick comedy," she'll say, maybe even in front of company. Right now this thought doesn't comfort me at all. After a couple bites, I put the roast beef back in its white bag and start on the tuna which turns out to be absolutely delicious. I take the top piece of bread off and examine the spread: white tuna, mayonnaise and little dark greenish stuff. Capers, I think, and I taste one just to make sure. How surprising that the toothy boy at the liquor store deli would think to put capers in the tuna. I start to call out the amazing news to Jule when my chest catches and I remember I've just caught her in bed with Kate.

"It's only a dream," I say to the cat who's lying on her back now near my feet, twitching all over. Her front legs jitter with electricity and then her mouth and eyelids begin to move. "You're safe," I whisper and then I begin to cry. Her back legs calm down and I whisper, "What is it? A dog or the vacuum cleaner?"

Then Jule sits down next to me. "She's gone," she says. I look at her as if I've never seen her before. She's wearing a sleeveless white blouse and khaki shorts. Her skin seems different, whiter and more delicate than usual. Her hair is slicked back and wet.

"You took a shower," I say. And then I begin to scream things at her because of the reason she had to take the shower. I tell her to move in with Kate if she's so wonderful. I shout sexual positions and body parts. "How long?" I scream.

"Not long," Jule says and I believe her. What else can I do? If I don't believe something the whole thing will unravel and nothing will be left.

"I want to go away from here," I say. "If I had a mother, I'd go home to her now." I want to ask her if she still loves me and why she did such a dangerous and careless thing. I want to go upstairs to my room and slam the door and just look out the window for days and days.

"Yeah," she says. "Not long and it won't happen again. That's the absolute truth. I don't want you to go away."

I don't go upstairs to my room. Instead, I look back at the cat and try to think of what to say next. The cat is lying there in the same position, breathing softly. It's important what I say because it'll be a sign of whether or not I'm going to forgive her, but right now I still don't know who she is. I look into Jule's eyes and what really hurts the most is that they're the same as ever, deep blue and kind of sad.

TATTOO

"Hurry up," Eleanor shouts at my bedroom window. She is outside loading the car and I am taking my time fixing my hair which is thin and needs a lot of work. Ten minutes before this the zipper on my pants broke so I had to start all over again getting dressed, which meant I had to repack my suitcase as well. Not a good omen, any of this, for beginning a two-week vacation with someone you've never travelled with before. I glance once around my bedroom with exaggerated nostalgia as if this is the last time I'll ever see it. Then I begin to wonder why I go anywhere. I'm anxious for a week before the departure date, it takes me four days to adjust to the new place and when I get home I invariably get sick.

But Eleanor is standing in my doorway now, smoking a cigarette. She is short with a round freckled face and lavishly curly gray hair. She is not afraid of anything. She has been married three times and has a tattoo on her wrist that she got on her last vacation. Supposedly it didn't hurt. It's of a butterfly because she's a Gemini, Eleanor has explained, and Geminis ride the breeze. I take that to mean that she doesn't stay with any one thing too long. She had it put on her wrist so she can cover it with the face of her watch when she's at work (she's an ophthalmologist not far from the university where I'm in administration). We met at a meeting of Adventuring Women, a group that organizes outdoor vacations for women who, for whatever reason, don't want to be with men. Eleanor's reason is that she is sick of them.

"Now hurry up, Nikki, or we'll hit the commuter traffic," she says. I'm moving slower than usual because it's so early in the morning and Eleanor is making me nervous.

"The zipper on my pants broke," I say. "Maybe we shouldn't go." As soon as I say it, I want to take it back. Eleanor's mouth twitches, just slightly, but enough to let me see I've hurt her feelings. "Oh, you know how neurotic I am," I tell her. "Don't pay attention to anything I say." I hate to belittle myself just to make Eleanor feel better, but it seems easier than telling her the truth, which is that I'm scared to spend a whole two weeks alone with her. We have a pretty nice friendship as it is; we talk on the phone once a week and take long walks in the mountains on weekends when it isn't rainy. Why push it? Spending a lot of time together is only asking for trouble. I'm a lesbian and she's not, so there's no romance, thank God. And no judgements either. She once said to me, "I envy you. Going to bed with a man is just plain stupid."

"Carry this, would you?" I say and hand Eleanor the Sportsac garment bag I bought for the trip. We're taking her car, a comfortable but small gray Toyota, so I've had to decide carefully what I'll need. I hand her the bag but I don't let go when she tries to take it. I stare into her green eyes for a couple of seconds. I notice for the first time that her left eye seems to be more brown than green and I wonder crazily if this asymmetry is what caused her to go into ophthalmology. She returns the look but then realizes her cigarette is burning her fingers and turns to find an ashtray.

"What the hell is wrong with you today?" she says, finally just grabbing the bag from me. "You having your period? I hope not. It's a mess bleeding on a vacation with hotel sheets and gas stations. I'm glad I'm through with all that shit." She walks downstairs to her car with my bag over her shoulder. The bottom hangs practically to the ground.

Everything in my bedroom except for a pair of sheepskin slippers is put away. I decide to leave them out so I can think of them, while we're hundreds of miles up the coast, waiting for me to come home. I walk downstairs and check all the doors and then go outside where Eleanor has just finished packing the trunk.

"You want me to drive?" I say to Eleanor who puts my suitcase in the backseat. "Wait. You like to drive, don't you?"

"Yeah," Eleanor says, getting into the driver's seat. I climb into the other side and put my seat belt on.

"Should I run back in the house and get some apples or water?" I ask her. "I didn't even think of it."

She starts the motor. "Don't worry about it," she says. I can see the butterfly on her wrist because she's not wearing her watch today.

"It hasn't faded at all," I say. The wings are bluish green and the body is red, outlined in black. It really looks like it belongs there, like it's a miraculous freak of pigmentation, not something put on with a needle.

"You ought to get one," she says. "A crescent moon, maybe or a scorpion. That's what you are, right?"

"What?" I say.

"Sign of the zodiac," she says. She speeds up to get through the yellow light and I push down on the floorboard with both feet.

"Yeah, November," I say. "I'm supposed to be sexy and vindictive. Fiercely demanding of loyalty."

"Where'd you find all that out?" she asks, like it's funny I should know that stuff.

"Somebody gave me a birthday card with it written on the inside," I say. Actually I'm pretty interested in astrology and I like being a Scorpio, even though I think I act more like a Libra.

"We couldn't be worse for each other," Eleanor says, laughing. "This vacation we're going to get you tattooed." The way she says it makes me feel like a head of range cattle. "You're going to come back from this vacation with a beautiful work of art on your butt," she says.

"Why my butt?" I say. All I can think of is the time my mother got me vaccinated and it hurt so much I didn't speak to her for three days afterwards.

"Why not?" Eleanor says merging neatly into the slow lane of traffic. "It's as good a place as any and it doesn't show, unless... ," she looks at me and winks. I think it's kind of mean to bring that up when she knows for a fact that it's been two full years since I've been to bed with anybody.

"But it's so permanent," I say. I'd heard they could take off tattoos but I knew the outline would still be there no matter what they did. "What if I change my mind later?" I can't imagine anyone wanting to tamper with their body. It's like saying you're God.

Eleanor runs her butterfly hand through her curly hair. "I think you should get a crescent moon with a little star in the concave part," she says, finally. "That fits you just right."

Eleanor drives as if we are in a tremendous hurry and after a couple of hours of strained reminiscences about terrible family vacations we stop at an ARCO for a fill-up and the bathroom. Eleanor buys an Almond Joy and I get a soft ice cream cone even though it's only ten o'clock in the morning. Then we get back in the car and start driving again. I begin to feel better about going on vacation. I pretend we're on our way to take a spring hike.

We talk about this woman, Roberta, whom we knew from our first Adventuring Women canoe trip. The thing about her is that she just married a man and on the canoe trip she was so homesick for a woman that the leader had to canoe her seven hours back to the parking lot where we had left our cars. Eleanor thinks it's a lot weirder than I do, but that's probably because she's so off men at the moment. I almost ask Eleanor if she's ever had any homosexual inclinations, but I decide we're on a vacation together for two weeks and why get into that?

At about noon we pass an old tourist attraction I remember driving by when I was a kid and we were going on vacation. It was a family-type restaurant, as I recall, and in front there was a recreation area for kids with slides that ran through the bodies of giant fiberglass animals. Sort of like a MacDonald's but bigger. For example, if you climbed up the elephant's back, you entered the slide at its head and shot out through the trunk. All that's left is an empty lot with a two-story gray/green dinosaur standing in the middle. Part of the dinosaur's skin has fallen off and I can see the wooden framing inside. Before I think to tell Eleanor we've sped past it. She's going seventy-five.

Finally Eleanor takes us to a truck stop restaurant. Without warning she just pulls off the highway and into the parking lot like that was our exact destination all along. It is four thirty in the afternoon and we're only an hour or so from the cabin we've rented on the edge of the Pacific Ocean. "I'm sick of driving," she says, "and I want some onion rings." We climb out of the car and stretch our backs. Eleanor lights her second cigarette of the day. She always seems to know what she wants which probably made it both easy and hard on all her husbands. I admire her for it. I hardly ever know what I want; all the possibilities have so many sides.

"You've been very nice about not smoking," I say. I put my arm around her and we walk into the restaurant.

There's a good solid feel to her and because she's about three inches shorter than I am, it's a little like she's holding me up.

"I don't notice so much when I'm driving," she says, dragging deeply.

We sit down at a booth next to the window and order cokes and onion rings and just as the waitress is walking away, repeating our order to herself as she finishes jotting it down, Eleanor calls to her, "Make that to go, would you?" The waitress, a large woman with jet-black hair the color of a piano stool, turns around and glares at us. The management has dressed her in a pink fifties waitress uniform that hits above her dimpled knees and makes her look like a joke. I think she is worried about her tip but when Eleanor smacks down two dollars, she seems satisfied and takes our order to the kitchen.

"I don't like this place," Eleanor says. "Too many men." I look around for the first time and notice about a dozen men, a couple at tables talking, but most of them solemnly smoking and drinking coffee at the counter, not even looking our way.

"Oh come on," I say to her. "Nobody gives a shit. Please let's stay in here. I'm just beginning to get over the sensation that we're still moving."

"I suppose you like the artwork," Eleanor says, lighting another cigarette. She points at the wall where a blonde dressed in a black bikini two sizes too small for her is drinking water from a garden hose. The cashier, a small, dark-haired woman, is ringing up a paunchy truck driver directly beneath the woman's rear end. "How would you like to be strung up like that, like so much meat?" she says.

"Of course I don't like it," I say, "but I'm on vacation and I don't want to get all worked up about every little sexist thing we run into." I lean back on the bench and feel proud of myself for saying exactly what I want to. I'd gone through a period of feminist rage a couple of years before and now, probably because of exhaustion, I've trained myself to look straight through the billboards, and magazine ads and everything else, like they're all just so much stale air.

"Little sexist thing!" Eleanor shouts. "Let's leave," she says and begins to stand up.

"No," I say, "please." I must be giving her just the right look because she stamps out her cigarette and then walks over and says something to the waitress. "Thanks," I say when she sits back down.

"Want to play a game?" she says. "Want to see how long it takes one of these assholes to get up and come over here and try to join us?"

"That won't happen, Eleanor," I say. "Everybody's tired. It's five o'clock on a Monday afternoon and all anybody can think about is getting home."

"They're thinking about sex and trashing women, take my word for it." She taps the table a few times with her index finger for emphasis.

"I hate the way you do that," I say.

"I've been around a lot longer than you and I've known a lot more men." She pauses. "And they're all the same."

"So what's it matter how many I've known if they're all the same?" I say. At this moment, the waitress returns with our onion rings and two glasses of water.

"You decided to stay," she says. "Good idea. The Interstate gets real bad at this hour. Last night on top of everything else somebody's car flipped over and burned up. We were stuck for ninety minutes without moving and I'm claustrophobic." She takes a bottle of ketchup out of her apron pocket and puts it next to the onion rings.

Eleanor bites into an onion ring and I begin to think about how you never know what people are going to come up with to be crazy about. Here is this perfectly normal looking waitress who hates closed-in spaces. "So what did you do," I ask her, "about the traffic jam?"

"Oh, I just got out of the car and walked around it a few times," she says. "It helped that I knew I wasn't really trapped. I mean I could of just left the car there and run down the off ramp any time I felt like it."

And Eleanor with her thing about men. And me with my... what? My phobia about being with anybody for more than a few hours at a time?

The waitress leaves and Eleanor pushes the plate of onion rings at me. She has already made quite a dent. "What are you thinking about?" she asks me.

"My parents," I say.

"Oh," she says. "Forget it." I take an onion ring from the plate and curve it through the little mound of ketchup Eleanor's put on the side. "I thought you might be homesick," she says, real seriously. I can't tell if she's making fun of me or not so I let it go. The truth is just at this moment I am missing my two cats who are probably staring squinty-eyed out of their cages at the cat hotel where I took them last night. I'd tried to tell the night manager their personalities but she looked so bored I just sort of trailed off and left the phone number of our cabin.

"She didn't bring our cokes," Eleanor says.

"I'll catch her eye," I say, for some reason feeling responsible. I turn around to see where the waitress is and I notice that the man three booths behind us is staring in our direction. Because there's nobody in the booths between us, he sees me looking and glances down at his plate. The top of his head is bald in a perfect circle about the circumference of an English muffin. I think of a target. "I don't see her anywhere," I say. "Just drink the water for now. She's bound to come over this way soon."

Eleanor is nervous about getting the cokes, as if she's worried about losing money on them or something. She smokes a cigarette with one hand and eats an onion ring with the other. I can tell she's not thinking about anything except where are those cokes.

"These are good," I say, biting into another onion ring. The batter is light and crispy and the onion tastes sweet.

"People write guidebooks about the best diner food to buy on vacation," Eleanor says, looking over to the cash register to see if the waitress is there. Then she puts her cigarette out.

"You on vacation?" a voice says. The balding man has suddenly appeared at the end of our table.

"No," Eleanor says, not even looking up. It's as if she sensed that he was on his way over. There is a silence. The man is trying to size us up. Not in a mean or sly way, but just if he should ask something else or go. Finally he smiles at Eleanor.

"Yes you are," he says. "I heard you talking about vacations as I was passing by. I'm on vacation too."

"She lives a couple of miles south of here and I live a couple of miles north. We meet once a week for onion rings half way in between," Eleanor says. Now she's looking at him with her jaws clamped together tight.

The man continues smiling at both of us. He has lovely large white teeth. He's wearing a light blue cashmere pullover and gray corduroy slacks and he reminds me of a guest conductor or a psychiatrist, definitely not a masher. I can't understand why Eleanor's putting us all through this.

"That was really an untruth," she says, straight at his white teeth, "intended to blow you away. We have all the company we need."

"I'm sorry," the man says. "I was just on my way to pay the bill and I heard 'vacation' so I thought we might exchange notes. I'm heading north to escape the smog for a month."

Suddenly the waitress comes up behind him, smiling, as

if she's terrifically pleased to find him there. She has the cokes. "I forgot your cokes," she says, moving around him so she can put them on the table in front of us. "Am I too late?" she says.

"Yes," Eleanor says and nods at the plate of onion rings which is empty.

"Are you joining them?" the waitress says to the man. "You want her coke?" and she puts one coke in front of my place and one to my right where he would be sitting. Then she puts the bill on the table. "Tell the cashier to take the cokes off the bill if you don't want them," she says and goes to check on another table.

"We're leaving now," Eleanor says, standing up.

"Of course," the man says. "I'm Don Peterson." He walks with us to the cash register. I stand to the side while Eleanor pays. I notice that she doesn't tell the cashier to take the cokes off the bill. "People always say that diners have the best food," Don says, waiting to pay behind Eleanor. "Somebody even wrote a guidebook about it."

I begin to feel sorry for Don Peterson and ashamed of Eleanor for treating him so badly. I begin to think that there's something wrong with me for being her friend. "Sounds lonely," I say to him, out of the blue, and he looks at me as if he doesn't remember who I am.

"What?" he says. Eleanor glares at me fiercely but I can't stop now.

"Going up north by yourself, to get out of the smog."

"It's what I want to do," he says, and leaves it at that.

Don Peterson has a convertible Mercedes and it is parked next to Eleanor's Toyota. "My one extravagance," he says, patting the door. "I've always hated the heavy libidinal thing Americans have for their cars but it's heaven to drive." Then he gets in, backs it out and waves at us. "Have a nice vacation," he shouts out the window as if nothing has happened, as if he just had a delightful talk with two women he'd never met before. We get in Eleanor's car and follow him out onto the surface road.

Eleanor is driving much slower than she was before we stopped. She merges into the middle lane of the freeway and stays there. Don Peterson's Mercedes is about five cars in front of us. "Men think we should be grateful for the interruption," she says. I look straight ahead. A huge bug splatters its guts on the windshield just my side of center. I stare at the yellow and red goo. Eleanor doesn't talk for awhile which is just as well because I can't seem to decide how I feel about anything.

Finally I look over toward Eleanor and it's like she's punched me in the throat because she's crying. Not hard but just enough that the tears are falling down her cheek and landing on her blue cotton shirt. I look away and stare at the squashed bug on the windshield, wondering what the hell I should say. I've never seen her cry before.

From the right, a four-wheel drive jeep, license plate TOUGH, cuts in front of us. I shout "Watch out!" just in time and Eleanor slams on the brakes.

"Jesus," she says. "The waitress was sure right about the traffic."

"Eleanor," I say.

"What?" she says. She's stopped crying but there are still little puddles of tears caught under her eyes. "You want to change your tampax? I did sort of rush us out of the restaurant fast."

"No," I say. "Actually I don't even have my period."

"I thought you said you did." she says. "I've been under that impression all day."

"I've decided to get the tattoo," I say.

"Hot damn," she says. "If we go down to the boardwalk right when we get into town, it'll have time to heal while we're still up here. We'll buy some Vaseline at the drugstore."

"But you got yours someplace else," I say, trying to re-member where she went for vacation last year.

"That's ok," she says. "These places have to be licensed. Besides, I'll check out the equipment, to see that it's sterile and all that. I won't let anything bad happen to you."

She turns toward me for a moment and one of the old tears slips down her cheek. She wipes it off with the back of her hand and smiles.

Suddenly I feel dangerously euphoric. The sensation sweeps over me that from now on all the messes in my life are going to be as just as easy to fix as this one. I say, "Well, get going," and without any hesitation she merges into the fast lane and all of a sudden, at seventy-five miles an hour, we're flying past everybody on the road.

AVALON

My psychiatrist doesn't look at me when he talks. Instead he fiddles with his flexomatic watch band or flashes on and off the expensive digital face.

"Express your anger, Jane. Challenge the problem head on. Confront, demolish, rebuild," he chants. He is big on healthy slogans in his modern high-rise office. "Be obnoxious, wreck the party, but don't clam up. You'll feel better afterwards no matter what happens."

He pauses so I can grapple with his words. He repeats them so I can hear them echo. Every week he takes me to my childhood and leaves me there and I think he does it for the money. I'm nearly thirty and he's extremely methodical. We could take forever to get to the pearl.

I call the psychiatrist to tell him that I have decided to stop seeing him. Then I hang up. I am extraordinarily nervous. He calls back to harass me.

"Why don't you come to your sessions?" he asks bitterly. "Come for one final session so we can tie things up."

He talks like a lover begging for one last chance. This is probably the best thing he has ever done for me. I feel grand and charitable and I agree. Then I begin to plan extravagant ways to spend his fees: trips, piano lessons, a velvet jumpsuit. I will at last be able to keep my dreams to myself.

I started going to the psychiatrist because of my relationship with men. He told me that I am ambivalent about men—love/hate, Mommy/Daddy, yin/yang, etc., etc. In these eight months my relationship with men hasn't changed—I am still stiff and somewhat ironic around them—but he has made me aware that there are other things wrong too. I have an obsessive fear of lingering cancer and earthquakes; I am insecure around people with authority; I overeat when I am lonely and I am often compulsively clean. I could go on.

In my carrel at the public library I notice that someone has written, "Make Love Not War," on the wall with fresh ink. I wonder where this person has been for the last decade, what war is being referred to. I imagine that the writer is a recluse and that it has taken years for him or her to identify with the anti-war graffiti scene. Now it is too late and the phrases are dead language. For a moment I feel better pretending I am better adjusted than the writer. It is a small and silly game and I am immediately ashamed. I write underneath, "The old must die and the young do die," a maxim my morbid Yankee grandmother used to call to me whenever I crossed the street. I think it lends a sense of inevitability and timelessness to the slogan above.

At our final meeting the psychiatrist is curt, then cold. We seem to be doing this for his benefit alone.

"I'm certain that you will be back soon," he says, "unresolved, and that my appointment calendar will be full by then." He threads his fingers in front of his mouth and stares at me.

I tell him that he is blackmailing me. He pretends to be shocked. I am challenging the problem head on, I say, what better evidence of my successful treatment? I enjoy being coy with him, flirting with his unhappy predictions.

"How about every two weeks?" he asks. For an instant I waver. Maybe the break is too final and I am more unstable than I think. Every other week?

"No," I say.

"How about a little medication then?" he asks. His voice is slippery and careful. "A little antidepressant." He takes out his prescription pad.

"No," I say.

I must try to imagine him naked or shitting. I am terribly afraid to say these things to him. "I need to work on it alone for awhile," I say. I am impatient for a direction to my life and he insists on taking me backwards. I must picture him as a small child before he can speak in sentences. Now he is fumbling for the first time with a sorority girl's underclothes. She is to be his wife but she will never really love him. She has affairs with functional illiterates. "Don't worry about it," I say. "I'm much healthier than you think. And I'll keep your number right by my telephone just in case."

"Goodbye, Jane," he says, shaking my hand as I leave. He looks past me into the waiting room. I am being forgotten. He burps. Then he calls in a sullen man with a small dog. I cannot help but look for a resemblance between us, this next patient and I, as if we are related through our psychiatric needs and treatment. And I wonder what courageous journey he is travelling, and how much further he has to go before he can finally rest.

I dream for the first time in my life about having a baby. It's born long and thin (I am not) and it speaks fluent academic English. I am very protective and she, my little girl, adores me. Our relationship seems to be based on mutual respect. We go to the beach and I teach her to build castles. She listens patiently with her little trowel dangling in her hand. I wake feeling great pride.

I spend hours planning the details of my fantasy pregnancy. My first child will be born on Catalina Island, in the five-bed hospital there so that she and I will be the absolute center of attention. The preparation and delivery will capture the steamy island imagination; we will all be one great extended family and the baby presents will be lovingly handmade.

I name the baby Avalon after the island's only town. She, of course, will be tow-headed and delivered through the Leboyer "Birth Without Violence" technique. No rough slaps, only dim lights and womby water for my sweet girl. Smug in my modern forethought, I am sure that there would be no need for psychiatrists if we'd all been born this peacefully. I wait each night now to dream of my baby's father, as if, when he is fleshed out, it will be some sort of sign.

Now that I am not going to the psychiatrist anymore I find that I have a great deal more time, particularly on the day before the session when I used to try to figure out interesting insights to share with him. If I'd told him my dream about Avalon he would have said, "I hear you telling me that you have creative impulses, Jane. I think your unconscious is telling you to return to your macrame" or "your calligraphy" or "your watercolors."

He could never be the father of my precocious, dreamy baby.

I take a part-time job at the local weekly newspaper organizing the subscription list, classified ads and billing. I have never worked before because my former husband had so much easy money. I spent most of my time then trying to dress well and understand him in all his misery. His name was Brian and he is dead now. He drove expensive racecars too fast, the result of a secret deathwish, I now believe. His death satisfied a lot of people because it supported the maxim "Money can't buy happiness." It satisfied the psychiatrist because it helped to explain my trouble with men.

In my new job irate subscribers phone me when their newspaper is not delivered or winds up in the newly mulched roses. I have no excuses. I do not use my real name.

"Circulation, Miss Harper speaking." I pick up the receiver with one hand while sorting names and renewal dates with the other. I have discovered in this job that I work extremely well with small details.

"I don't know what you people are doing down there but I've missed my paper three weeks in a row," shouts the woman on the other end. "I want all those copies and my money back by tomorrow. What did you say your name was?" Formerly I would have wept or cowered if someone spoke to me like that. Now I can deal with the hostile public adeptly, even two calls at once.

"Miss Harper," I say. These people like to personalize the opponent.

"Well, Miss Harper," she smirks, "speak." This woman has a gift. She has made me a docile animal, a dachshund.

"We do often have trouble with the post office," I say, although I am not making excuses. "I will send you out the back copies today with your thirty cents and double check the mailing list." I am not terribly sorry but I enjoy doing my job well.

"All right," she says, slightly mollified. "I realize that you have very little control over these complications. You are merely a cog, after all." I laugh slightly on the other end to show her I know my place.

The newspaper office is really very pleasant. I bring my lunch in a sack and eat it at my desk while I work. There is a lot of work. Too much to be called part-time, but the newspaper has very little money and I don't need much anyway on account of my husband's generous bequest. The paper has liberal leanings and high ideals and constant trouble with advertisers. Often I have seen the editor in tears. There is nothing any of us can do about it but we all know the paper is doomed to financial failure. Because of this unspoken certainty, we are often swept up in a marvelous bravado, missing deadlines and typos. Still, the final product is far better than most. I keep all the back issues in a drawer at home so I can remember this time in my life, later on. Although I am not involved in the editorial side of things, I see myself as the steady bridge between readers and writing, between the thought and the consequence.

The newspaper fails. I am despondent. Everyone else gets new jobs almost immediately. I am too miserable to think of myself. My new skills seem hardly applicable to anything else anyway. For the last six months I have barely thought about terminal cancer or earthquakes and I am able to talk to most men as equals. I can feel my workday self-confidence slipping away like warm, rich blood as I sit in my house looking backward. I become addicted to masturbation, infertile and lonely as I am now.

One cold night, I am almost always cold these days, I jerk awake to remember my last dream. I am perspiring and the sheet is wrapped around my waist like a sloppy cummerbund.

In the dream I am sitting in an outdoor cafe, sipping champagne with a dark, handsome man who looks like he might be a model for some musky male cologne. He is obviously fascinated by me and plays with my little finger across the table as if he were testing fine fabric or memorizing something. I enjoy his touch because it is so gentle and limited. He seems not to require anything of me beyond my presence at his table. Our conversation is filled with little

sighs and grunts directed at each other with gasping passion. Soon it becomes evident that we are to make love, because of the constant insistent movement of his fingers. In
ridiculous uninhibited dream fashion, I am ready to climb
under the coffee table with him, my skirts over my head,
using my napkin to cover the cold cement. I have a long and
wrenching orgasm in my sleep.

The next morning I decide that I must get another job immediately. I am too preoccupied with phantom pains and
loneliness. I buy the newspaper and circle twelve want ads,
two employment agencies and a downtown women's job
resource center. Then I type up a resume so convincing and
intelligent that I am sure I will be offered employment as
soon as I apply. Under "Career Objective" I type:
"Administrative assistant in a position of responsibility and
human contact. Opportunity for advancement required."

In fact, I am offered three jobs, a record according to my
employment counselor. I want very much to think of her as
a wise and gifted teacher with the keys to my future at her
generous disposal. Instead she is a thin, wispy blonde
woman who works mostly on commission. She is very
happy with me. She, of course, wants me to take the high-
est paying job, with the loan company, which I was offered
because I passed the mathematical test requiring speed and
precision. If I take the job I will be involved in helping the
company foreclose on loans, repossess houses and furniture
and appliances, a vindictive opportunity, it seems to me. It
is 4:45 and I have to decide immediately. The other two jobs
are slightly more interesting but the counselor presses me so
convincingly that I begin to believe she is thinking of my
own good.

"Wait," I say. "I'll tell you in the morning."

"But," she says. She stamps both feet under her desk,
staccato. She seems so desperate for her cut that I fear she is
actually hungry or underhoused. "The job will be gone by

then. It's an employer's market nowadays." I look away
and she plunges at me as if I were a fat chicken. "You're not
so special. What's wrong with you? Are you playing with
me?"

There are weekly charts on the wall with pastel bars indi-
cating counselor standing. My counselor's pink bar is the
shortest one of all. I can feel her public humiliation. I must
go.

Outside it is winter and nearly dark. I walk quickly to my
car in the empty parking lot. When I take out my car keys I
feel boiling breath on my ear.

"Just do what I say and you won't get hurt."

For a moment I am crazy and I think that the employment counselor has called in rough accomplices in her
desperation.

"Yes," I say, "I'll take the job. Sure, sure." There is
something sharp near my spine. "Who are you?" Suddenly
I feel certain that this man is going to hurt me. I scream.

"Shut up," he says. He shoves me past my car across the
parking lot to an empty field thick with weeds and bushes.
He pulls me down next to him and offers me a cigarette.
Silently we smoke. The scary unreality of this scene makes
me hopeless and faint. I begin to shake during this lull. I
turn to look at him. I have to look deep to see him but he is
young and tired underneath his wino's clothes. His pants
are stained and baggy and his eyes are red.

"Don't stare," he says. "I'm sick so don't tell anybody
about this. The last time somebody told I had to go out and
do it again."

I start talking. I say anything, fast so nothing can happen
but my words. I tell him about my dead husband, my
house, my psychiatrist, the newspaper, my job interviews. I
tell him things I've never told anybody. I repeat my favorite

quotations. "Success always demands one final effort, one more great play," "No man is an island." I am lying on my back and he is raping me.

"Enjoy it," he says. It is important to him to know my pleasure. I realize that I have never had sex with anyone I didn't think I loved. This sex is ludicrous and mean and terrifying. I look into his face and fake orgasm. I keep my eyes open as he moves in me to remind myself that he is a human being. He is the man in my dream cafe and we are making a baby. Avalon. I dig my nails into his back, pretending passion. He will kill me if I stop talking. If I stop talking, I won't wake up.

Suddenly he lunges in me and then rolls off onto the grass. He looks up into the dark sky breathing heavily, his arms across his chest. I am alone with my body waiting for the final unbearable violence. The ice pick is on the grass between us.

"Was that good?" he asks. "Did you really come?"

"Yes," I say. "Wonderful." I will say anything. I will tell him I love him. I can barely move my lips; they feel frozen. He bit them, I think, and smashed them against his teeth.

"Do you want me to kiss you down there?" he asks. He is leaning on his elbow toward me. He is much younger than I thought with just the bare traces of a beard. It occurs to me that this may be his first time.

"No," I say. He may kill me but he will do it anyway. "I am dressed now and very tired. I came already so there is no use." I sit up and he moves toward me. He will kill me now, I think, and the scene is set in my mind forever like a flash of pure light. I shouldn't watch. It isn't real. My heart stops absolutely and my skin is rigid. I believe that I desire this, more than anything else in my life it will complete me, but I am afraid.

He raises his arm and then brushes the leaves off my hair and back. He does this very gently. "Thank you," he says.

He is not going to hurt me at all. He looks around the field.

"Stay here for five minutes while I get away." He is up on his haunches.

"Wait," I say. I don't know what I want. He spots the ice pick and shoves it in his back pocket. I feel a fleeting tenderness for him. He didn't hurt me.

"You should get help," I say. "You can't keep doing this."

"Ok," he says too quickly. "I'll go to my priest."

"Promise," I say. I am crying.

"Yeah, sure," he says. "I'll go to my minister." And he is gone and I am alone with my humiliation. I am still alive.

When I get home I lock the house and then I vomit until there is nothing left but heaving and empty shudders. I stay up all night because I can't stop moving. There is no one I want to call and nothing I can do. I am caught somewhere between night and day.

I decide that I should go back to the psychiatrist for awhile. He will be glad to see me after such a long time. He will ask me about the experience, my reactions, and he will draw parallels between them and my childhood. He will try to make me feel better and that is something. He will sit behind his desk playing with his watch instead of looking at me and I will attempt to make sense out of my life. If he asks me I will tell him what I know is the truth. I will tell him that I am glad I wasn't killed. I will tell him that I wish I had taken the ice pick and eased it right into the rapist's resting heart.

My Father, the Novelist

"I had many dreams when I was young," my father says to me. I look at him with affection and wonder if he knows that he is being a pure cliche, the middle-aged man cataloging his youthful dreams, his secret desires. We are eating a nice dinner which I have spent very little time preparing. His is getting cold. The recipe is deceptively easy: soup, rice, chops in a Dutch oven, but the finished product looks like I really made an effort. The appearance is all that matters anyway because he will barely taste his. He did not come for the food.

"I could have written a novel. I still can," he continues after a couple mouthfuls of rice. "I could take a month off work and write a novel anytime."

"That's ridiculous," I say, but not meanly, because naive optimism is exactly his charm. "You can't write a novel in a month."

"Yes I can," he says. "I've been writing it in my head for years. Putting the words on paper would be mechanical."

I try to imagine this to see if I can take him seriously. I've never read much of his writing except for a letter to the editor of his favorite skin diving magazine about an inner-ear operation he'd had and a true account of a bizarre tax case which was rejected by the op-ed column of the local newspaper. The description of the inner-ear operation was humorless and sincere. My father was angry when he read it because they'd taken out all the stuff about anesthetics and bedpans, the parts he thought were funny. The bizarre tax case for which he was the accountant wasn't all that bizarre.

Now he is eating very slowly because he is talking about all the things he could have done.

"What would you write your novel about?" I am interrupting his fantasy of a breeding kennel where he would raise virile but friendly labrador retrievers.

"Oh my life, of course," he says. "It would sell for sure. It's got everything: death, love, sex, disappointment."

I could have guessed the topic but still I am surprised. This is something I hadn't known about my father, that things which don't work out disappoint him. He has always seemed so ready to substitute something else—another woman, another sport—so that there's never an unsettling pause. He is extremely sporty although rather uncoordinated. He began jogging immediately after he realized that his tennis would always be lousy. Now when he plays tennis he's simply "out-of-practice." He began dating my stepmother two weeks after he left my mother. Now he is leaving my stepmother for someone even better.

"Eat," I say to him suddenly. I sound like his mother or his wife and he looks at me, startled with misplaced recognition.

"It's very good, Angela, really terrific. How do you keep them so moist, these pork chops?" He takes a big bite of the chop and chews noisily. "Your house looks great. I'm glad you're taking good care of yourself."

"Everything's fine," I tell him. "It's an easy recipe. Listen, I don't know why I said that. I don't care if you eat or not, really."

My father once told me a sly parable about sex and marriage. "An ancient Chinese told his son," my father began, "if you put a small bean in an empty dish every time you make love your first year of marriage and then remove a bean every time you make love after that, you will never see the dish empty again."

I was fifteen at the time and I was slow to work out the mathematical point. He had to repeat the thing several times. Finally, understanding, I found the story unspeakably depressing, partly because it seemed so personal a statement of my father's experience with marriage. I don't think he found it depressing at all. I think it made him feel very wise to appear to be a cynic.

"Everybody has disappointments," my father is saying. "That's why details are good to put in a novel. People identify, they think you are speaking directly to them. My disappointments are these: my father dying young. That was unfair. He died, you remember, of TB, a curable disease nowadays." He pauses, perhaps to search for subtleties. I know, of course, about his father dying. In fact, both parents died when he was four, of TB, probably infecting each other.

"Do you think it's too unbelievable for a novel, both my parents dying at that age? Too sentimental for the modern reader?" he asks me.

"It depends on how you treat it," I say. "I never really think about it except I'd like to know if he would have kept himself in good shape." My father flexes his bicep absently, gripping his fork.

"My second disappointment is that I'm uncoordinated," he says. "I've lifted weights, I've pole vaulted, I run, I scuba dive, but I know in my heart I'm mediocre. My diving students surpass me in weeks. I run with women and they lap me. Usually they pace themselves, but I know. I can hear their even breathing."

He hangs his head and I remove our plates although he has left half his dinner. I put the dishes in the sink and I soak the Dutch oven. Soon he will begin on his third disappointment. It is nine o'clock.

I bring my father a cup of coffee. He is leafing through a magazine reading the cartoons as if they all have double meanings. He laughs loudly and jabs the page with his finger.

"The street sign says 'Walk,' he explains, "and the cripple throws down his crutches to cross the intersection. Ha. That's so terrific. Do you get it?" Since the tale about the beans and the dish I think my father assumes that I get very little.

"Yeah, sure," I say. "The joke turns on the cripple taking the sign literally." I feel like an idiot, explaining the workings of a joke.

"Right," my father says as if he is mildly surprised. "Good."

"So what else will be in your novel?" I ask him.

"Well, I'll have to include your mother in the early chapters," he says. He squints as if he is straining to remember anything. The first marriage was so wrong and so long ago that I can hardly blame him.

"When we were first married it was wartime. She was pretty, strong-looking. I thought I was going to have to join the army so we were married before either of us was out of school. She had a terrific backhand." He stops to think. "We played in some tennis tournaments, mixed doubles, but it didn't work out. Everyone directed all their shots at me. She developed a fine poaching game but it wasn't good enough to save us." He looks down at his hands for a moment. "She wasn't a good loser, you know, Angela. It made things sometimes very awkward." I wait for him to go on. I am aware that my father has had very little experience describing relationships and his use of the tennis analogy seems particularly hopeful. But, he says nothing more.

Finally, I realize that there is nothing more. His analogy was simply a statement of events. This then will have to be the secret of his marriage to my mother, the bad sport, which lasted fourteen years and ended in a bitter and constant dispute over alimony payments. My mother now lives miles away at the beach and will not speak to my father except in court. She is the only person on earth who thinks he is ill-intentioned.

"Of course," he continues, "I'll treat it humorously in my novel. A battle of the sexes type situation. Cary Grant and Katherine Hepburn in tennis shorts. Harmless but clever verbal sparring between the sexes and in the boudoir."

I cannot imagine writing a novel and changing things that really happened so completely. It seems cowardly and perverse. I consider pointing this out but my father is busy replotting the next major event of his life.

"About this business with your stepmother," he says. "It occurs to me that it will dovetail perfectly with the athletic comedy of the first marriage. I'll portray it as a tragic romance, perhaps with *An Affair to Remember* twist. Beauty, terminal illness, moonlit boat rides, a favorite bar where the piano player does 'our song.'"

"But didn't you just find someone better?" I ask. I know this is true because I have had long talks with my stepmother who is bereft. He found someone who is slightly younger and quite a bit richer. She plays even better tennis than my mother did but, with surprising wit, the new woman refuses to play with my father. The relationship seems to have possibilities.

"Well not better exactly," he says. "Better for me, you might say. She'll be like a mother to you, Angela." He is leaning toward me with excitement. "And you'll remain close to your stepmother and it will be like nothing has changed except for the living arrangements."

I decide not to question this version of the situation. A man who reads Camus for fun, a man who starts each day as if nothing is going to go wrong and can actually remember only the good things, is practically immune to reason anyway.

"And how will you end your novel?" I ask him.

"I haven't mentioned you," he says after a moment of serious thought. "A daughter. A bright young woman with a solid foundation in the humanities. Our philosophical talks, the things you learn from me regarding the nature of adulthood. Pivotal scenes from your life so far, particularly dwelling on my influence. My unswerving support as your original model of masculinity. You as my hope and gift for the future." He stops to see if I like the idea. I take his hand in mine. Of course it is a preposterous fantasy and almost totally self-centered, but still it is a sweet thought. I would love, in fact, to be able to believe it.

"This is a very sincere use of the father/daughter bond," I tell him. "Still, it's kind of a funny way to end a novel based on your romantic experiences. Maybe the public would be disappointed by this final, homespun theme."

"That's a good point," he says immediately. "I could tie the daughter in with the third relationship instead. Daughter as matchmaker. Daughter as sad to see father lonely. Daughter, in last chapter, as maid of honor."

"Yes," I say. It is too bad to have to lose my star billing so quickly for the sake of art, but probably it is best this way. "That sounds more like it. I think that would give the novel a more even flow." Suddenly, I feel a little bit like crying.

He leans into the couch and puts his hands behind his head. "Well," he says. He is clearly pleased with himself. In one evening he has written himself another life that is simple and clear, a life free from hidden motives and unattainable dreams.

"It's been a great night, Angela," he says and he smiles at me as if I know just what he's talking about.

STRANGER

Although there is only one dentist in the office, a compact man with a passion for fly-fishing, there are three patient rooms, each set up with chair, drill and an aluminum spit bowl at eye level around the edge of which water circles eternally like some kind of life force.

"You're a good patient," Dr. Inadomi says to Valerie, patting her on the shoulder as he reaches for something near the drill. Valerie doesn't mind his tone even though she is certain she has at least five years on him. Lately, she's started thinking about getting old and now she looks down at the leathery skin on her hands and notices they are beginning to look a lot like her mother's.

"Bite down on this for a few minutes to let the cement set," he says and places a small pine stick between her teeth. Then he adjusts the timer and leaves the room. He often works on three patients at once with the help of his assistant, Laurie.

While Dr. Inadomi works on your teeth, he usually describes the trip he's planning or the trip he's just taken to fish for trout in Idaho. Earlier today, while the smell of burning enamel was rising into Valerie's nostrils (she was being prepped for a crown—another scary sign of incipient old age), he told about how his wife always photographs his catch before she throws it back into the stream. He said he never keeps more than he can eat even though the stream is stocked. He was proud of that. And he was proud that his wife was so good at photographing fish with the polaroid. She knew how to capture the fight in their eyes and the light on their scales and she knew how to remove the hook from their jaws without tearing anything. After she returned the fish to the stream, his wife waited for Dr. Inadomi to catch another. Valerie wanted to ask what his wife did while she waited. Did she crochet or knit or read? But Valerie couldn't talk because the dentist's hand was in her mouth drilling her tooth into a tiny thing, just big enough to hook the crown to.

And now, because the partitions between the patient rooms stop about a foot from the ceiling, Valerie can hear the voices next door clearly. Suddenly she recognizes them and this makes her shiver as if she were standing knee-deep in one of Dr. Inadomi's trout streams. The voices she hears are the dentist's, of course, and that of the woman she's loved from afar for more than two years.

"Such a good patient," Valerie can hear him say to the patient next door.

"You say that to everybody," the woman says. "You just said that to the patient over there." She laughs Katherine's husky laugh, and Valerie finds that she can't seem to stop thinking in these damn fishing analogies. Katherine's laugh is like a warm sweater you'd pull on after a day of fishing in a clear mountain stream. You'd be sitting by the fireplace in your cabin and you'd feel a breeze from the window and you'd shiver and your lover would bring you this sweater which you would pull over your head and snuggle into like a hug.

Now she can hear Dr. Inadomi saying, "We'll take x-rays first, Katherine. Then, if you have any cavities we'll fill them."

Actually, that's the way Valerie puts herself to sleep every night. She fantasizes about romantic places she would visit with Katherine if they were lovers or about to be lovers. In these stories, the time right before they first touch is usually the most exciting, the moment when they both know they want to, but somebody still has to work up the nerve to go first. Usually this is when Valerie falls asleep.

"You skipped the part about the drilling," Katherine says to the dentist. "You remember how I hate that."

It sounds to Valerie as if Katherine is flirting a little, but not very seriously. She does that a lot in the faculty room if the two of you are waiting for the coffee to drip; she acts as if you and she have a private joke. Cocking her head to one side she'll say something kind of intimate and then wait for a reaction. She does it with everybody; people seem to be interchangeable to her. She'll stand by the microwave and ask, for example, how your cramps are, real quietly, maybe putting her hand on your arm and you'll start to answer and the microwave timer will go off and that will be that. She'll have forgotten she asked and you feel stupid to bring it up again. This is probably, Valerie thinks, the reason she is so taken with Katherine. If she could get Katherine's full attention just once, maybe she could finally let her go and think about something else.

Her favorite fantasy is the one where the two of them are at a weekend education conference. The fantasy usually goes in two parts: in the first, Valerie is sitting in a chair on the woodsy deck when Katherine comes up behind her and asks if she can join her to talk. Slowly, deliberately, Katherine takes her hand as if it is the most natural thing in the world. The second part happens later (if Valerie's still awake); Katherine comes to her dormitory door (the whole thing is set at a rural retreat house) at night and says she'd like to get to know her better. The lovemaking is thrilling, partly because they have to be so quiet in the twin bed next to the plywood wall.

It's not love that I feel, Valerie is thinking; it's something much more complicated. And simple. For one thing, she hasn't been with anyone since Gloria, whom she met almost three years ago at the Women's Center Lesbian Rap Group, and who turned out to be a bisexual. Gloria told the group that she wanted to be a lesbian but she couldn't find a woman who would be nice to her. Strangely, almost immediately, Valerie found herself being late to dates and forgetting to bring her wallet and after six weeks she told Gloria she couldn't see her anymore, that she'd met someone more stimulating. She hadn't. She'd just felt this powerful desire to hurt Gloria's feelings. She'd known from the beginning that she would.

Maybe, today, it will be possible to slither out of the dentist's office without Katherine seeing her. Maybe everybody just takes turns being victim and victimizer.

While she waits for the dentist to come back, Valerie turns her head to the right and examines the painting on the wall. She is trying to think about something other than Katherine—the wavy gray hair, the soft, round breasts under the pullover sweaters she wears in cold weather, the way her eyes crinkle at the edges behind her glasses. She is trying to stop thinking about all the women she has loved this way, obsessively, without success. She is trying to understand what the hell is wrong with her.

She stares hard at the painting. All the rooms have paintings by this one artist. Many visits ago Valerie realized that they are all different and yet all the same. Forested nature scenes, at first glance, with native Americans and animals wandering through. On second glance, there's a secret you're supposed to find. Each painting is hiding something. The aspens are camouflaging pinto horses and brown-skinned men wearing white. The rocks in the stream, taken in groups, form stony, impassive faces. The standing bears are actually men wearing furs and pelts. In this particular painting, the sky and water look just the same; the water reflects the sky so that the clouds seem like stones. This afternoon, the artist's facility annoys her. She squints at the signature. Bill Reynolds. Valerie is certain that Bill Reynolds has an answer for everything.

"We'll just take these and develop them," she hears the dentist say. And then he calls for Laurie. She hears the soft rustle of Laurie's polyester pants suit as she walks down the hall to the pick them up.

"How are you doing?" Laurie stops to ask her. Valerie nods mutely because of the stick in her mouth. Laurie bends to wipe some saliva from the corner of her mouth with the napkin that's lying on her chest and Valerie feels a ridiculous welling of tears in her throat that shames her. She lives alone. She watches Katherine at work. She chooses her outfits, her jewelry, thinking about what will appeal to Katherine. And now she is listening to her talking at the dentist's office in the cubicle next to hers.

Last month Valerie taught *Pride and Prejudice* to the juniors and when they got to the part where Darcy and Elizabeth finally meet at Pemberly—dark, moody, intolerant Darcy jumping wealthily over the boxwoods to meet Elizabeth—Darcy was suddenly short, stumpy Katherine in a sensible blue corduroy wrap-around skirt moving energetically towards her in the high school parking lot, finally. Valerie was so moved by the vision that she burst out with "Doesn't that scene just make your heart race?" Luckily it did; this was the honors class and the kids really got into the characters they read about.

"Finally," Maureen Murphy sighed. "I mean I knew it was going to happen but when it finally did... "

"That's called suspense, stupid," Annie Sterling said and the class laughed because everybody knew they were best friends. The discussion made Valerie feel better; it allowed her to feel hopeful about Katherine. It was just suspense she was going through, not unrequited love, not the absurdity of a thirty-five-year-old woman pining away after a married mother of five.

Dr. Inadomi takes the stick from Valerie's mouth with the hand that had been in Katherine's mouth just two minutes before. He sneezes into his face mask. "Excuse me," he says. "I'm getting a cold. I could be getting a cold or it could just be an allergy. Bite down again, please. The cement hasn't quite dried. I don't think I'm contagious behind this." Valerie watches him breathe in and out behind the aqua mask he's wearing, pulling the mask into his mouth a little each time he breathes in. She can see the outline of his lips and every black hair in his eyebrows. She closes her eyes. "We're almost done," he says. "You've been such a brave patient." He pauses. "I think you know Katherine Collins, the patient next door." His hand is in Valerie's mouth, running a polishing instrument over the surface of the crown. "I just noticed from your charts that you teach in the same place." He raises his voice to call over the partition. "This is Valerie Bloomfield over here, Katherine. You know her, don't you?"

Something in Valerie's heart jumps. She sees a trout leaping high in the air. For a crazy moment, she thinks maybe Katherine won't answer, maybe won't remember who she is. Love me, Katherine, she thinks. Love me. At least remember who the hell I am.

"So you're skipping the faculty meeting too," Katherine laughs flirtatiously. "Are you almost done? I need someone to hold my hand while I get drilled."

They go out to dinner at a Mexican restaurant around the corner from Dr. Inadomi's office. Katherine's idea. She says that her husband and the two kids who still live at home are at a slo-pitch softball game in the park and she's always

wanted to get to know Valerie better and so isn't this perfect? Isn't this just propitious?

"Where do you live? We live on the edge of the canyon,"
Katherine is saying. She motions to the waiter for more
chips and salsa. She's already finished two bowls by herself
and two margaritas. She's acting giddy, like a teenager with
a fake ID. She's obviously a woman who rarely gets out on
her own. Valerie is still sipping her first margarita because
it's so strong and now she thinks they ought to order if
they're ever going to get home. The first part of the evening
went almost too fast. She wanted to remember everything.
The drive over (they left one car at the dentist's),
Katherine's perfume as Valerie helped her off with her wool
coat, the way everyone seemed to look at them as they
walked to their table. But now, things are going too slow.
They both work tomorrow and Valerie doesn't have anything to say because Katherine seems to be doing all the
talking.

"We've lost three cats to coyotes in the past six months.
You might ask why we keep replacing them." Valerie
hasn't wondered that. She's been visualizing the coyote
grabbing the cat by the throat and shaking it back and forth.
She's been thinking about how the cat felt. She has a big
gray cat named Stranger whom she talks to and brushes
every night but who is never satisfied. Stranger is always
under her feet, rubbing on her ankles, trying to trip her so
she'll feed her something wonderful. But Valerie can never
figure out what Stranger wants. She's tried chicken livers,
ground round, cream, and, of course, every kind of canned
food there is, but nothing works. Stranger eats enough to
stay alive and spends the rest of the time working on
Valerie, crying and looking hungry.

"Are you listening, Valerie?" Katherine says. There is
now a plate of ceviche on the table, little pieces of white fish

with flecks of tomatoes and green onion swimming in the vinegar marinade. Valerie can't remember anyone ordering it.

"No, not really," Valerie says. Suddenly she feels exhausted and depressed. She doesn't care about trying anymore. She'll tell the truth. She's given up on trying to be a good listener or whatever the hell Katherine wants her to be. Telling the truth feels almost exciting; it feels kind of like the sting of sex between her legs.

Katherine seems surprised. Valerie notices that she is looking especially pretty tonight. She's let herself go a little bit because she's had so many kids and a husband and teaches high school on top of that. Something has had to go. But, it is like she is still in charge of herself, even if she is a little bit gone, like she knows what's happening and it's ok with her.

"I talk too much when I'm nervous," Katherine says and takes Valerie's hand.

"It's ok," Valerie says. "Sometimes I get too quiet." Katherine squeezes Valerie's hand and looks into her eyes for a few moments. Something peculiar is happening, that much is clear and Valerie suddenly feels sort of dizzy.

When Katherine speaks again, the ceviche has been taken away and the four people sitting at the table next to them have paid their bill and gone. "I found out Bob has been having affairs," Katherine says. "I won't tell you how I found out, but I did and I've been pretty upset."

Valerie presses Katherine's warm, pudgy hand sympathetically and stares at the table, wishing she were home now, in her nice big bed with Stranger, watching the news. She notices that her tooth aches too, because of the cold margarita, and for this, she blames Katherine.

"May I come home with you, Valerie?" Katherine is saying, her eyes brimming with tears. "I'd just like not to face him tonight."

"You want to make him jealous by not coming home?" Valerie says, taking her hand away. Now that she's decided to tell the truth, she's having fun with the conversation.

"No, no, that's not it at all," Katherine says, but Valerie can tell that's definitely part of it.

"Yes it is," Valerie says. "I have a fold-out couch you can sleep on. It's ok to want to make him jealous. Sometimes these things take drastic measures."

The restaurant seems quiet all of a sudden. Valerie looks at her watch. It's nine-thirty and most of the other customers are gone now because it's a weekday. Two waiters are laughing together in a corner, while a third is sitting at an empty table putting little packages of sugar into the holder.

"I'm attracted to you," Katherine says, tentatively, vulnerably.

"No," Valerie says. "You're kidding. I'd never guess that at all." And as she says this, she feels a surge of blood rise to her face and a space begins to open up inside her, a space that's warm and soft.

"You're a lesbian, aren't you?" Katherine says. "I mean, I've always just assumed you were."

"You have?" Valerie says. She can't believe she's having this conversation. With Katherine of all people. Valerie has always taught in a dress and heels. She always wears large earrings. She made it a rule years ago never to go out within a twenty mile radius of work. "Why did you?"

"Lesbians always seem more sure of themselves, I think, in their bodies. They don't slouch like they're ashamed of being women. You act like that, Valerie. You may not know it but you do."

"Well, thanks," Valerie says, sitting up straighter. She is fighting the desire to take Katherine's face between her hands, to smooth the wrinkles out of her forehead with her thumbs.

And, suddenly Valerie is remembering something she

saw when she was five. She's remembering the time she walked into her mother's study in the middle of the afternoon. She'd been looking all over the house, calling her name for ten or fifteen minutes. By now, she was beginning to cry. She went to the garage, climbed into the station wagon and honked the horn three times and then she remembered to look in the study. When she walked in she saw her mother sitting on the couch with her arms around a woman she recognized as Mrs. Martin, a neighbor.

"You don't come in here unless you knock," her mother shouted at her. "You little bitch," Mrs. Martin hissed. Mrs. Martin was busy buttoning up her blouse. "You forget that you saw us," her mother said. "We were having a nice talk." "I always said she was a little bitch." Mrs. Martin pushed her out of the way to get to the door. Mrs. Martin was kind of heavy and smoked lots of cigarettes. She pulled out a cigarette and lit it before she walked home. She blew a mouthful of smoke in Valerie's face and her mother didn't say a thing. She was scared of her mother after that and the Martins moved away. She was scared of her mother and she was a little bitch. But she never told a thing.

"Are you attracted to me?" Katherine is saying. "You watch me at school sometimes, I think. Unless I'm mistaken. I could be mistaken." She seems miserable, Valerie thinks. And desperate. Married for a hundred years to this heel and she's trying to have her first affair. A woman probably seems easier than a man. And Valerie's obviously been transparent in her infatuation and the meeting at the dentist's office seemed like a message and now there's this moment, this terribly awkward moment. Valerie can't decide what to do. She breaks a tortilla chip into tiny pieces, buying time.

She's thinking that it's like the paintings in Dr. Inadomi's office. Or it's like trout fishing. The world is full of signs and symbols. Everything means something but Valerie can never be sure what. She's caught Katherine but she ought to throw her back. You look at the situation one way as easily as you can look at it another. It's like the water circling the spit bowl; it's like finding her mother with Mrs. Martin in the study.

"What are you thinking about?" Katherine says. "They're closing up and we ought to pay."

And then, like she's looking into a perfectly accurate crystal ball, Valerie knows exactly what's going to happen. She's going to invite Katherine to her apartment where Katherine will pet Stranger and comment on how beautiful she is, how blue her eyes are. Stranger will jump on her lap and purr loudly. Valerie will give Katherine one of her nightgowns, will kiss her lightly on the mouth and will invite her to join her in bed. There, in a rush of breath and heat, she will make love to Katherine, as if her life depended on it and she'll sleep without the need for any fantasies at all. But, it won't be until long afterwards that Valerie will realize how little she actually wanted her. It won't be until long afterwards that she'll realize that Katherine wasn't who she wanted at all.

Paula Martinac   Carla Tomaso

About the Authors

Paula Martinac is on the editorial board of *Conditions* and is the editor of the anthology, *The One You Call Sister: New Women's Fiction* (Cleis Press, 1989). She lives in Brooklyn and is currently working on a lesbian ghost story.

Carla Tomaso lives in Pasadena, where she teaches English at a girls' high school. Her stories have been published in *Common Lives, Lesbian Lives* and anthologized in *Unholy Alliances* (Cleis Press, 1988).

About the Series

This volume launches a new series for Seal Press, designed to celebrate and instigate new voices in lesbian short fiction. We encourage lesbian writers who have not yet had their stories collected in book form to send us their work. We are also interested in hearing from poets, playwrights and novelists who work only occasionally in the short story form. *Voyages Out* will be published every year; each volume will feature the work of two writers.

Please send six to fifteen stories for selection to Barbara Wilson at Seal Press, 3131 Western Ave #410, Seattle WA 98121.

Other Lesbian Titles from Seal Press

LOVERS' CHOICE by Becky Birtha. $8.95, 0-931188-56-3.
Wonderful stories by an important Black lesbian feminist writer.

THE THINGS THAT DIVIDE US: Stories by Women, edited by
Faith Conlon, Rachel da Silva and Barbara Wilson. $8.95,
0-931188-32-6. Stories that explore issues of racism, classism and
anti-Semitism.

GIRLS, VISIONS AND EVERYTHING by Sarah Schulman. $8.95,
0-931188-38-5. A sexy, rollicking novel set in New York.

BIRD-EYES by Madelyn Arnold. $8.95, 0-931188-62-8. A
stunning novel of a teenage girl struggling to escape a mental
institution.

MISS VENEZUELA by Barbara Wilson. $9.95, 0-931188-58-X.
Collected stories by a well-known lesbian author.

THE DOG COLLAR MURDERS by Barbara Wilson. $8.95,
0-931188-69-5. Pam Nilsen solves the murder of an anti-
pornography activist. New.

SISTERS OF THE ROAD by Barbara Wilson. $8.95, 0-931188-45-8.
Pam Nilsen looks for a teenage prostitute. Second in series.

MURDER IN THE COLLECTIVE by Barbara Wilson. $8.95,
0-931188-23-7. A lesbian and a leftist collective merge—to
murder. First in the Pam Nilsen series.

HALLOWED MURDER by Ellen Hart. $8.95, 0-931188-83-0.
Sororities can be deadly—Jane Lawless goes after the murderer.

NAMING THE VIOLENCE: *Speaking Out About Lesbian Battering*,
edited by Kerry Lobel. $10.95, 0-931188-42-3.

LESBIAN COUPLES by D. Merilee Clunis and G. Dorsey Green.
$10.95, 0-931188-59-8. The definitive guide!

SEAL PRESS, founded in 1976 to provide a forum for women
writers and feminist issues, has many other titles in stock: fiction,
self-help books, anthologies and translations. Any of the books
above may be ordered from us at 3131 Western Ave, Suite 410,
Seattle WA 98121 (include $1.50 for the first book and .50 for each
additional book). Write to us for a free catalog or if you would
like to be on our mailing list.